SAMANTHA

A RETELLING OF SHERRI BY MAX COLLIER

W.B. FORD

For Beverly

1

WHEN THE MAIL arrived that morning, the contracts were there. Brooks Erickson knew what the envelope contained the minute he saw it and he smiled. The weeks of sweating and doubting were over. He restrained himself by waiting until he was back in his apartment before he tore open the envelope. He glanced briefly at the documents and lay them aside, unfolding the accompanying letter. As he had expected, the publisher wanted revisions and changes. That would mean a few weeks of additional work, but at least the main hurdle had been cleared.

After he had read the note, he began to look more favorably upon the book that had prompted it. The novel was his third to be accepted. But it never failed to amaze him that he could create something that others considered interesting and enjoyable. Writing seemed to come effortlessly to him, the words flowing from his fingers with such ease that at times he wondered if any creation of his was an honest literary effort. But as it had happened before, the publisher's mixed praise prompted him to look at his work in a new light. Maybe he had written better than he had thought.

He threw aside the letter and laid back on the couch, stretching his long legs in front of him. He smiled secretly to himself, his arms behind his head. He grabbed his iPhone and punched in his friend's phone number. Aaron usually was sleeping at that hour and resisted waking.

After a while Brooks heard an indistinct male voice faintly respond. "Yeah?"

"Wake up, lover," said Brooks. "There's good news today."

"Oh. It's you." Aaron groaned. "What the hell. Why are you calling me at this time of day?"

"I heard from my publisher."

The voice became more alert. "No kidding! I guess that means they think your novel is another *War and Peace*."

"Not quite, but they're willing to gamble on it."

"Okay, congratulations. Now can I go back to sleep?"

"Hell, no. We're going to celebrate," Brooks said.

"Man, you're out of your mind. It's practically dawn."

"It's nearly noon. Anyway, I don't mean right now. I called so you won't make other plans for tonight."

"Who makes plans?" Aaron replied.

"Will you celebrate with me or not?"

"Okay, okay. Who's picking up the tab?"

Brooks answered, "Depends on what you're drinking. You going to bring along Joann?"

"For you?"

Brooks laughed. "She's yours, not mine."

"Not anymore. She walked out on me last night."

"What did you do this time?"

"Do we have to talk about it now? It's too early. What do you want me to do, find you a chick?"

"Get off it. You're not the only one who cultivates females."

Aaron boasted, "I don't cultivate them. I plow them—straight and narrow."

"Who did you sleep with last night?" Brooks demanded.

"Nobody. I got drunk. That stupid broad…"

"So that explains your mood this morning."

"Okay, so I'm not a laughing boy. Can I go back to sleep now?"

Brooks said, "All right. I'll pick you up about eight tonight."

"Okay, okay," Aaron said as he ended the call.

Brooks continued to hold the receiver in his hand after Aaron hung up. He could understand his friend's lack of enthusiasm. They had become acquainted a number of years ago when they had discovered that they were fellow writers. They had spent many a night discussing their art, but the difference between them was that Brooks worked steadily at his writing while Aaron was content to philosophize about it and labor at it only when the inspiration hit him. The results had been that Brooks had had two novels published with minor success while Aaron was still working on his first. Aaron had been extremely enthusiastic about the publication of Brooks' first book, but now with the acceptance of the third, he had sounded practically indifferent.

Aaron's jealousy was to be expected, Brooks thought. The guy was like many other people who usually were happy about a friend's initial success, but not quite so delighted if the good fortune continued.

Brooks and Aaron had often argued about the latter's envy, Brooks trying to get Aaron to put more time into his craft. Brooks' point was that Aaron was too concerned with his career of glass-emptying and girl-chasing to devote adequate time to complete his novel. However, they remained friends in spite of the continuing dispute.

Brooks began to pace the floor.

He guessed that for a proper celebration that night they should have girls along. Aaron probably would not be much interested in discussing the book and in any case Brooks did not particularly want to spend the evening talking shop. But he did not want to spend it with Gail, either. She was much too quiet when sober and too garrulous when drunk. Ten days had gone by since he had seen her, yet that had not been enough time to erase the memory of their latest date. She had become drunk, had begun to talk, and must have poured out a million words before she had fallen asleep.

Even after he had bedded her down, she had continued to talk. He had been wholeheartedly pleased when he had awakened the next morning and found her gone.

If there were to be a woman with him that night, she would have to be somebody entirely new, somebody with an unknown past and an unknowable future.

As it turned out, Brooks found just such a companion. He picked up Aaron shortly after eight. Aaron had slept himself out, and already had gone to a liquor store for a bottle of Pinot Gris, which was properly chilled by the time Brooks showed up.

"Wine is a hell of a base for a celebration," Aaron complained, lifting his glass. "But I'm nearly broke. Anyway, here's to book number three and all the others to come. Have you signed the contracts yet?"

"There's no hurry. I've got some revisions to make."

"Man, you're really traveling. Three of them," Aaron said, smiling. "How many more are you going to write?"

"Who knows? Eight, ten, twenty? I figure I will keep at it until I've written the well dry or until I have ten or twenty million stashed away from when they turn my books into movies."

"Have any Hollywood producers made you an offer?" Aaron asked with surprise.

"No, but maybe someday they will. Maybe they'll eventually get down to scraping my part of the barrel."

"What you need is to put more insight in your books. Your characters should become more involved with living. There's not enough depth."

"I'm not a profound writer, Aaron. I'm more of a commentator than a philosopher. I've learned to practice my craft within the limits of my own capabilities. That's what you should do. Then you could give up your job at the shoe company and concentrate on writing."

"I'll get there, man," Aaron said. "What say we get this party under way? I feel like really letting loose, but not here."

"Want to go to the usual joint?"

"I don't know. Joann hangs out there. We may run into her."

"So what? Think of the fun you'll have making up."

They downed the last of the wine. "Come on," Aaron said. "Let's shove off."

They found the place crowded, and the customers more than lively. The two friends were jubilant. The atmosphere at the tavern was perfect for a celebration. Brooks and Aaron stood at the bar, listening to the flamenco guitarist. Every now and then Aaron would wander away to inspect the women in the crowd. He was not having his usual good luck with pickups, however.

"I don't know what's happened to these chicks," he said disgustedly to Brooks. "They've all shown up with dates tonight."

"The night is still young. If you pick them up now, you'll have to foot the bill for getting them softened up," Brooks said jokingly.

Aaron put his hand on his pal's arm. "Wait a minute. I think we've struck pay dirt."

Brooks followed Aaron's gaze to two girls who had just arrived. One was a small elf-like creature to whom Brooks once had been introduced. He vaguely remembered that her name was Pam. The other girl was a head taller, blonde, and beautifully built. He had not seen her before, but she was striking enough to interest any man.

Aaron pushed away toward the pair and grabbed Pam's shoulder. Brooks saw her glance up at his friend, smile, then laugh. She turned to her companion and introduced the two. The girl smiled faintly, but in the dim light Brooks could not tell much about her expression. His arm linked with Pam's, Aaron led her toward Brooks' station at the bar. The blonde followed behind.

"You've met Pam before, haven't you, Brooks?" asked Aaron.

"Only briefly," Brooks replied. "Good to see you again, Pam."

"This is her girlfriend, Samantha," said Aaron, gently prodding the girl toward Brooks. "And Samantha, this is Brooks Erickson. He's David Foster Wallace's greatest competition."

"You're a writer?" The blonde girl said.

"We're celebrating the acceptance of his third book," Aaron volunteered. "He is a writer. One of the best," he added forcefully.

Samantha smiled indulgently at Aaron, then looked casually at Brooks. "Is that true?" she asked.

"Aaron won't associate with anybody but the best," Brooks said. "May I buy you a drink?"

"Thanks. I feel like a rum and coke tonight, with lime."

"Good hot weather drink, I'm told," Brooks said, motioning to the bartender. "It's supposed to cool you off."

"Who wants to drink to cool off? I thought the purpose was to get hot," she commented.

Up close the girl appeared younger than when Brooks had first seen her. Samantha's face was unlined, as flawless and fresh as a baby's. Yet there was no incorrectness about her expression not in keeping with the youthfulness of her features. Brooks was not sure what lay behind the look. It could have been disdain. He was intrigued by it. Why should a girl so young be contemptuous of men?

"It seems Pam and your friend have disappeared," she said, gazing about the room. "I guess that leaves just us."

"Do you have any objections?"

"It's all right with me," she said indifferently. "One man is as good as another."

"Good? At what?" Brooks was more intrigued than hurt by her indifference. "Flagpole-sitting? Tightrope-walking? Marijuana smoking?"

She smiled with real amusement for the first time. "The Constitution says all men are created equal."

"Then how come Aaron is four inches shorter than me and that man over there outweighs me by seventy-five pounds?"

"Don't take the founding fathers so literally," she said, frowning slightly. "They meant equal in rights and opportunity. And psychologically. It's that last bit—male psychology—that levels men for me."

"You're getting involved in an argument you can't win. You know that."

"Maybe I can't win the argument, but what I say is true, nevertheless. All men, if you ask me, think and behave in the same ways."

"You sound like a man-hater," Brooks remarked.

"What's to hate? Men are walking conceits who live by caprice and urge."

Brooks laughed. "What programs have you been watching?"

"I don't waste my time with TV," Samantha said indignantly.

Brooks made an elaborate pretense of closely examining each of her shoulders. Samantha watched him, her velvet-brown eyes hostile. "I'm just checking for chips," he said. "I seem to have knocked them both off."

"Sorry," she said. "Nothing personal, you know."

"I hope there's nothing deep-seated about your attitude."

"Why? Why should you care how I feel?"

"I hate to see anyone so young be so cynical. It's bad for the morale of the human race," he replied.

"Are you some sort of idealist?" she said with a trace of sarcasm.

"I may not be, but I like to think that I am. There's hope in idealism."

"Hope is a thing with feathers," she said. Her words caused Brooks to sit back and re-evaluate her. The words came from a quote from the poem he knew, but the fact that she had memorized them changed his concept of her. Samantha was beginning to evolve as a personality. She was not just a girl to ply with liquor until her resistance was gone.

He asked, "Where did you get that line?"

"What's wrong with it? I happen to like it." She was definitely defiant in her tone.

"Nothing's wrong with it. But hearing Emily Dickinson quoted in a cheap saloon is unusual."

"Well, when you come right down to it, hope belongs in a saloon. It classes with liquor—something bewildering. Something to blind yourself with." She suddenly laughed out loud, throwing back her head so that he could see the gleaming white crowns of her teeth and the pink inner surfaces of her mouth. The site was strangely exciting to him. "We're being awfully intellectual with each other for such a short acquaintance," she said.

"Is that so bad?"

"Well, it's just not done. It's like hooking up on the first date. We're supposed to get to know each other first. Hey, there are Pam and your friend at the table. Why don't we join them?"

"If you insist." Brooks followed her through the crowd.

Aaron cast an appraising eye at Samantha as she and Brooks arrived at the tiny table. But since Brooks held her elbow in a more or less possessive manner, he turned his attention back to Pam.

The two couples stayed at the bar until about midnight, when it became impossibly crowded. They piled into Brooks' car and drove to Pam's apartment.

They tiptoed past the owner's house. Aaron exaggerated gestures invoking them to silence caused the other three to crack up. They muffled their laughter and, after Pam unlocked her door, rushed into the room. They fell down on the couch and chairs, guffawing loud enough to wake the sleeping landlady.

Pam drew forth her meager store of booze and made screwdrivers, mixing the vodka with orange soda instead of orange juice. At first taste, her guests grimaced, but nevertheless they drained their glasses. Aaron and Pam became intensely interested in each other after that and curled up together on the couch. Samantha surprised Brooks by dropping down on his lap—he was in possession of the only armchair—and coupling her open mouth with his, she sent her tongue on a desperate foraging expedition as if it were starved and living in enemy territory.

The intensity of the kiss caught Brooks off guard. For a moment, after her lips left his, he stared at her as if nothing like that kiss had ever happened to him before. He remembered the whiteness of her teeth and the pinkness of her tongue when she had laughed so heartily in the tavern, and he recalled her quotation about hope. Suddenly he was looking at her with new awareness. She was no longer a strange young girl with a cynical smile, but an irresistibly attractive woman. She was hardly conscious of the warm flesh of her buttocks in his lap, the firmness of her waist under his hand, the moist scarlet of her lips so close to his. Her brown eyes looked down into his blue ones as if trying to see into his mind, to peer into the very depths of his soul. There was an intensity in her gaze that fascinated as well as alarmed him.

Without taking her eyes from his, she brought up her hand and touched the line of his jaw with her fingertips. "They're going to start doing something pretty soon. Do you want to watch them?"

He knew she was referring to Aaron and Pam, and he brought his hand up to the lithe thrust of her heavy breasts. "Not particularly," he said. "You want to go over to my place?"

She lowered her head and her lips again fastened on his.

"Does that answer your question?" she said, lifting her head.

"I think it does," he said, conscious of the softness of her breast against his palm. He glanced out of the corner of his eye at Pam and Aaron. They were a heaving complex of tangled limbs and mussed up clothing.

"If we mean to miss the show, maybe we better clear out right now," Samantha said.

She slipped from his lap and took his hand in hers, drawing him to his feet. He followed her like a docile dog, pausing long enough to turn out the light, leaving in darkness the clutching pair on the couch.

It was only a few minutes before they arrived at Brooks' apartment. Yet during that interval, Samantha seemed to have undergone a change of heart.

Once inside the door, he immediately put his arms around her. She gave him her mouth readily enough, but held herself stiffly, unyieldingly, so that just the tips of her breasts touched his chest. Her thighs and stomach touched him not at all.

"Is something wrong?" Brooks asked, drawing back his head to look at her.

"No. Why?" She moved away from him and lit a cigarette before sitting down on his couch.

"Maybe I've deceived myself, but in Pam's apartment I got the distinct impression that you were all for this."

"So, I changed my mind."

"Oh, you're one of those," Brooks said in disgust.

"What do you mean by 'one of those'?" she asked, mimicking him.

"The tease type."

"Why? Because I won't roll over and give you what you want the very moment you want it?"

"No," Brooks said, more loudly than he had intended. "Because you led me to believe you would."

"I'm sorry," she said, looking at him gravely. "I thought I wanted to when we were back at Pam's place. But now it doesn't seem right."

"What the hell?" Brooks said. He stamped into the kitchen to make himself a drink. He figured he would not bother about her, changed his mind, walked to the entryway, and leaned against the door jamb.

"Do you want a drink?" Unsmiling, he asked.

"Do you have any rum?"

"Nothing but bourbon."

"It's too hot for bourbon."

"Who drinks to cool off? he said, repeating the remark she had made earlier in the evening.

"*Touché, mon cher.* All right, I'll have one. Over ice, with just a little water."

He brought her the drink and sat down on a chair opposite the couch, and watched her, annoyed yet still wanting her. She was a well-developed girl, large-boned and big-breasted. Her stiffness of posture suggested inner tension. The structure of her face, he thought, was strikingly attractive--prominent cheekbones, aquiline nose, firm chin, and full mouth. Her face, like her body, was the kind not easily ignored.

"What time do you have to check in with Pam?" he asked after a while.

"No special hour. I'm on my own. Do you want to get rid of me?"

Brooks shrugged.

"You're angry, aren't you, because I won't hook up with you."

"What will we do now, analyze why you won't? Kick the subject around until we're sick of it?"

"Have you anything better to suggest?"

For more than an hour they argued, sometimes quietly, sometimes angrily. Finally in exasperation, he threw her out.

He had to. By that time the sight of her exquisite body had so powerfully excited him that if he had not gotten rid of her, he probably would have ravished her.

2

THE DAY after Brooks had met Samantha, he shoved the publisher's letter in his pocket along with the notepad and started out for a nearby park. He did not particularly want to work in the park—it would be full of distractions—but he would enjoy sitting there and meditating. Brooks seldom got out in the sun because of his practice of writing indoors and every day. He felt justified in taking the time off only when he hit a problem that needed to be thought out. Then he believed it permissible to take a long walk or spend an hour or so in a park.

Sitting down on one of the park benches, with the hot spring sun burning down on his bare arms, Brooks opened the publisher's letter and reread the suggestions. There were three areas indicated for revision. He began to write an outline of what he remembered of the specific scenes, adding marginal notes about things he would say if he were writing the scene for the first time. He was not sure whether the ideas he jotted down were those he already had used or were new. He would check his first draft.

He did not work long on the revision, however, before Samantha's image interrupted his thoughts. When he became conscious of her intrusion, he was at first angry, and he muttered a few uncomplimentary words describing her. He tried to push his memory of her into the back of his mind. The night before had been most unsatisfactory, especially as a celebration. He had not been able to sleep after he had demanded that she leave his apartment. His restlessness had been caused not so much by unappeased desire as by humiliation. She was too young and too gauche to be affecting him so strongly, he had thought—and the thought returned to him now as he sat in the park. After all, he was an experienced thirty-five-year-old man. Samantha had not been his first woman...he corrected himself. Rather, she would not have been his first if he had been able to get her into his bed.

He had enough intelligence to write three books that others thought enough of to buy. The first had not caught on too well, but by being prudent with the proceeds, he had managed to sustain himself until the second had been accepted. That book had been a little more successful; his agent had even talked of a possible sale to the movies, although nothing had materialized. The royalties from the second book had been sufficient to enable him to save some money. This had made him feel secure enough to take more time with the third.

Brooks had struck out on his own immediately after leaving college. He had selected Boise as a place that was as good as any in which to write. He had known nothing about the community before he selected it other than that it was an old river town rich in history and tradition. After he had moved here, he had taken a job with an abrasives manufacturer until he'd broken the ice with his first novel.

He had remained in Boise after landing that first book, although he had kissed the abrasives firm goodbye. He had been glad to be rid of the backbiting cliques among the employees of the company. His literary success, limited as it was, had made him a little proud, and he had regretted that he had no family with whom to share his happiness. But he had been lionized by his circle of friends—a circle that included Aaron, to painters of abstracts, a lesbian poetess, a dabbler in ceramic crafts, and a jazz clarinetist who had a connection for marijuana. With the exception of the musician, Brooks was the only one of the group who managed to make a living at his chosen profession. That made him noteworthy. The others did not like his books because they were conventional. But he was published, and though to a degree they might begrudge him his success, they still respected it.

Brooks believed that in his association with the group, he had seen enough of the wild and sensual aspects of life to armor him, to inoculate him against yielding to an attractive female face and body per se. Thus, the fact that Samantha's image kept intruding itself was all the more annoying. He wondered for a time whether it was the fact that she had rejected him that made him think of her. But she was not the first who had turned him down. He had immediately proceeded to forget the others, yet for some reason Samantha stuck with him.

It was mid-afternoon when he walked out of the park and returned to his apartment building. He was astounded to find Samantha sitting on the top step, waiting for him.

His first reaction was anger. He stopped on the sidewalk and glared. "What the hell are you doing here?"

"I wanted to see you again."

"Why? So, you can tease me? Go on, take it to some of your other acquaintances." He moved past her into the building, walked up one flight of stairs and unlocked his apartment door. She was right behind him and followed him inside.

"I've read your books," she said, sitting down on the arm of the couch.

"When? This morning before breakfast?"

"I went to the library early. And I'm a fast reader." She smiled at him. "I like them. You have compassion."

That stopped him. He felt his annoyance and anger dissipate. "You want a drink?" He asked gruffly.

"You know, your friend called you a rival of David Foster Wallace," she remarked, ignoring his question. "What did he mean?"

"He meant I wrote about dark spots in our culture."

"I didn't notice much of that."

"Moral dark spots."

"You didn't come to condemn them in your books. You wrote about them as if you like them."

"I hate the morally sick, but it doesn't mean I can't feel sorry for them."

"What do you think I am?" she asked quietly.

"What do you mean? How would I know anything about you?"

"I'm like one of your characters."

"So, what moral disease are you afflicted with?" Brooks asked sarcastically, not sure if he wanted her to leave or to stay. He sat down in the chair with his drink.

Samantha said softly, "You don't like me very much, do you?"

"What do you want from me?" Brooks asked, unwilling to let her direct the conversation toward him.

She shrugged. "Maybe something wonderful."

"I tried to give you that last night, but you refused it. Remember?"

She was staring at him out of her velvety brown eyes. "I think you'd be good for me."

"I'm not a doctor. I'm a writer."

"But I don't need a doctor. I need someone who can understand me."

"That's a switch. I thought the current opinion was that men were incapable of figuring out themselves, let alone women."

"Don't be nasty, Brooks. I'm sorry about last night. I would have given myself if I could, but something told me not to." She rose and walked toward him. She stood in front of him and looked down, smiling sadly. "We could do it now, if you wanted to," she said, fingering the bottom button of her sleeveless blouse.

He was suspicious of the proffered gift.

"Why is this afternoon different from last night?"

"I know you better now."

"How could you know me better overnight?"

"I've read your books. I know you as well as I would if I had lived with you for ten years."

"Don't give me that. My books aren't autobiographical. They're pure fiction."

"An author can't help but reveal himself in his work," she said. "Everybody knows that."

"Well, I'm the exception," Brooks said.

Samantha suddenly sank to her knees and put her arms around his waist, resting her blonde head against his chest. "Don't throw me out again," she pleaded. "I'll sleep with you. I'll do anything you want me to."

He tangled his fingers in her ponytail and pulled her head back so that he could look into her face. With deliberate brutality, he asked, "Am I supposed to just go wild over that offer? Have all the others told you how good you are or something? Are you a special treat?"

Her eyes were closed and her lips twisted with pain. Although he could not know it, his words had cut to the most sensitive depths of her. "Help me," she said through clenched teeth. "Please, help me."

"Like this?" He asked savagely, thrusting his hand inside her blouse and grasping a firm, warm breast through her bra.

"If that's what you want, yes."

Suddenly he felt sorry for her. He realized that he was simply venting upon her the anger still boiling in him because of the frustration and humiliation of the night before. But obviously she was apologizing. She wanted to make amends. He lowered his head and pressed his lips gently to hers. "How can I help you?" he asked.

"By knowing me as I know you. By looking upon me as a woman and not as just a slut."

Brooks slid from the chair, sat beside her on the floor with his arm around her waist. "I never thought of you as I slut," he said. "Even though I picked you up in a bar, I didn't think you were slut."

"You acted as if you did. I sat on your lap and kissed you, which immediately made me a whore, as far as you were concerned."

"Oh, no. Samantha, I thought you wanted me. And I certainly wanted you." He stroked her hair. "That's all there was to it."

She has turned on her hip and their lips met. Her arms went around his neck. Without thinking, Brooks tightened his hold on her waist and pulled her to him. Slowly they fell back on the carpet without breaking contact, her legs parting slightly. He fumbled with the buttons of her blouse. She grabbed hold of one side of the material and yanked it violently. The button shot loose and her bosom burst through. Her breasts were heavy, round, and alive.

"No bra?" he mumbled.

She was in no mood for jokes. She arched her back, baring herself to him. He lowered his mouth to the creamy, pink-tipped mounds. She gasped as his lips moved along her flesh. With one hand she clutched him. With the other she pulled at the zipper of her skirt.

"Here, here," she said, taking his fingers and pushing them under the loosened waistband, down across her bare stomach. A slight moan came from her throat as his fingers caressed and explored. Her hips arched from the floor.

Brooks had to loosen her arms around him with his hands so that he could draw back from her. For a moment she lay with her eyes closed as he rose to his knees beside her. But when she opened them and saw him unbuttoning his shirt, she sat up. Her breasts quivered as she hooked her thumbs inside the waistband of her skirt and panties and slid them together down the full size and along trim legs. She kicked the clothing aside, lying back with her eyes closed, the gentle dip below her ribcage rising and falling with her rapid breathing.

Then Brooks was at her again, his lips brushing across her collarbone, his hands stroking along that soft skin of her inner thigh. She touched him, her fingertips sliding across his nipples, down to his stomach and to his loins.

It became more than he could withstand. As he settled his body on hers to ease himself, she clasped him to her not gently or lovingly but aggressively, as if driven by a need even more overpowering than his. Her fingernails digging into his shoulders goading him on like spurs. They're love, suddenly, had become some sort of contest, as if she were putting her will against his, her bodily strength against his. He drew upon all of his powers of control to keep up with her. For a time, he was able to outlast her, even though after the first convulsive threat of her hips she did not relent but struck wild rhythms with her thighs. Brooks strove to meet her demands. At last, when her body arched convulsively still another time, he let himself go limp. Samantha realized she had won. She gave a cry of triumph and collapsed.

For a long while after he had rolled from her, Brooks lay with his eyes closed, letting his heart, lungs, and mind return to normal. Then he felt Samantha's hand seek his chest, and he opened his eyes and turned his head to look at her. Her eyes were misty, and she smiled affectionately. He could see she was a little astonished by him.

"You're not through, are you?" she said.

He thought she was taunting him for it did not seem possible that she could not have been fulfilled. He had, he thought, outperformed himself. Certainly, he had never felt called upon to exert himself to this extent before, and the results should have been enough for her. He began to wonder just what he had let himself in for by allowing her to make use of him.

"Are you some sort of marathon dancer?"

"I can dance all night," she said laughingly. "Or all day, as the case may be. You did very well, though."

Brooks grunted and looked away from her, shedding his eyes. "If you feel that way about it, give me a few minutes."

"You're not kidding me, are you?"

"Not many girls could call my bluff about a thing like that."

She leaned over and kissed him.

For a long moment he held her in his arms, then tilted her head back and smiled at her. There was an intense expression on her face. Her lips glistened redly. "We'll see how expert you are this time," she said. "I hope you've had your vitamins."

At first merely a contest, now they're love became a battle, a Thermopylae of sex, in which each tried to vanquish the other. There was no frantic groping or striving, but detached control as if they had been studying war manuals on how to reduce an opponent to a state of full surrender. The struggle seemed to last an eternity, with Brooks pausing each time a spasm shook her. He would rest until her eyes were opened, and then his determination would return. When the bout finally ended, they collapsed together, their bodies slippery with sweat and their lungs about to burst.

Brooks raised up on his elbows and looked down at her face. Her lips were parted, her eyes closed peacefully. Her nostrils flared slightly with her heavy breathing. Perspiration matted her hair near her forehead. Her features were so relaxed that there was hardly any age or character to them.

Wearily he pushed himself away from her and went to the bathroom. He turned on the tap in the shower and climbed under the spray of cold water and shocked himself back to normalcy by the touch of icy cold liquid against his red-hot flash. He let the water stream over him for a while, then he stepped out and dried himself, wrapping the towel around his hips before returning to the living room.

Samantha was sitting in the big stuff chair, her skirt thrown over her shoulders as if it were a cape. The garment covered her breasts, but it failed to conceal her thighs and hips. She sat with her legs crossed. She was resting her head resting against the back of the chair. There was a look of respect in her eyes as she gazed at Brooks. She smiled weakly and asked, "May I use the shower, too?"

"Be my guest," he said, turning toward the kitchen before she had a chance to rise. He had no desire to see her walk naked across the room. At the moment her body was too familiar. He no longer wanted to be reminded of the debauchery to which her flesh had driven him. Yet he did want to know the girl better. This time, he would not send her away.

He mixed two tall gin drinks as Samantha showered.

Brooks found the humidity in Boise to be unbearable.

The dampness seemed to retain the heat so that the temperature would drop only a few degrees at night. The weather would continue that way for a week or more at a time.

He was blessed with a small balcony just outside of his living room and made a practice of sleeping there on very warm nights. But in the afternoon, when the temperature was in the high 80s and the humidity even higher, a tall cold drink, no clothes, and a towel wrapped around his waist was the only way to beat the heat. Of course, when he could afford it, there were air-conditioned cocktail lounges to which he could go cool off.

Brooks took Samantha's place in the stuffed chair. When she returned from her shower, she also wore a towel wrapped around her hips, retaining the light cotton skirt over her shoulder to hide her breasts. She saw the drink on the coffee table and sat down on the couch behind it. She picked up the glass, took a long sip and set it down. For a while they sat with neither speaking, both absorbed in their own thoughts.

"Nobody ever did that to me before," she said suddenly, not looking at him. "Nobody that took me that far."

"Are you complaining?"

"I don't know. I shouldn't, I guess." She said it so seriously that her tone caught Brooks' attention.

"You want to go at it again?"

"You mean you could?" she said in disbelief.

"You want to try?"

She shook her head. "Not now. I must have time to think."

"About what?"

"About me, you, us. But mainly me."

She was beginning to confuse him and Brooks did not like to be confused by the girls with whom he bedded. He preferred his females simple and uncomplicated, concerned primarily with the actions of their bodies, not their minds. Samantha has ceased to be the haughty, disdainful, slightly cynical girl the night before. She had become less sure of herself. Her shifts in mood and personality amazed and troubled him.

She was not looking at him, but continued to sit on the couch, her legs crossed, exposing large portions of thigh beneath the short towel around her hips. She turned the glass thoughtfully in her fingers, her face sober, her eyes turned inward.

Finally, she looked at him. "I don't think I like you," she said, and she did not smile.

"You mean you're disappointed?"

"No," she said. "It's something you wouldn't understand."

"Try me and see. I'm not entirely stupid."

"I couldn't explain without telling you about me, and I'm not sure I want to do that."

"You sound very melodramatic."

"I don't mean to. It's just that I don't particularly like to talk about personal matters. Why don't we let it go with that?" She resumed her haughty role of the night before, smoothing down the skirt thrown over her shoulder to make sure that the fabric covered her breasts. "Were you kidding when you said you could go again?"

"You want to find out now? You didn't a while ago."

"I think you're boasting." She smiled challengingly.

He stood up and approached her.

There was determination in her eyes as she slipped out of the towel. She shrugged the skirt away from her shoulder, exposing her breasts. As he stood over her, looking down at the beauty awaiting him, she rose and wrapped her arms around his hips pulling forward so that he had to brace one knee on the couch to retain his balance. She rubbed her cheek against his torso and kissed him.

He stroked her hair gently as she caressed him, and after a while he tried to pull away from her, to press her down on the couch. She resisted and clung to him, her nails digging into his flesh. He let her have her way for a moment longer, then tore himself away from her searching lips. He forced her down and fell upon her. Samantha grasped him passionately, as if she hadn't ever been taken before. Then the fierce and intense battle began anew. She seemed determined to drain him completely of his strength.

This time the contest was a draw.

3

BROOKS DID NOT SEE Samantha again until several days had passed. When he thought about getting in touch with her, he realized that he did not know her last name or where she lived. He called Aaron to ask for information but received nothing new. Aaron had not seen Samantha before that night at the bar, he explained. But he promised to ask Samantha's friend, Pam. Aaron had not yet called back.

Brooks sat in his living room this particular afternoon trying to analyze why he missed Samantha so acutely, why he wanted to see her again as soon as possible. The other women with whom he had made love before had not interested him greatly; sex had been the only thing shared. But with Samantha the situation was different. He kept thinking of her repeatedly as he worked on the revisions of his third book. The preoccupation exasperated him. True, she was young, vibrantly beautiful. He wondered whether his fascination stemmed basically from her physical attractions, along with her tremendous appetite for fulfillment. Certainly, she approached lovemaking with more enthusiasm than any other woman he had met. Still, he could not accept sex as the primary appeal. Sex was important to him but did not rule him as it did so many men.

Maybe he was drawn to her because of her contradictory personality.

One minute she was sweet and loving; the next, she was cold and withdrawn. Samantha seemed a deeply troubled girl. Brooks always had taken an interest in mixed-up people, especially when they were as intelligent as Samantha was. How such people approached their problems and dealt with them was the meat of his novels.

Samantha obviously had a problem and just as obviously was unwilling to talk about it—at least not to Brooks. But it challenged him. It made his need to see her a compelling thing. Did she miss him as much as he missed her? Hardly, he thought. Otherwise, she would have gotten in touch with him.

His musings were interrupted by the doorbell.

Throwing open the door, he saw Samantha standing before him. She was wearing faded blue jeans, a man's white shirt, and leather thongs on her feet. Her corn-yellow hair was pulled back in a saucy ponytail.

"Are you receiving?" she asked.

Brooks pulled her into the room. "Where the hell have you been?" He slammed the door shut. Then he seized her and drew her to him.

"I've been avoiding you," she said, and kissed him.

"I gathered as much. Any special reason?" His arm around her waist, he led her to the couch.

"I wanted to see if I could," she explained. "Avoid you, I mean."

"You sound as if I'm some drug you're afraid will hook you."

"That's exactly what I'm afraid of. I stayed away to see just how much of an effort it would be."

"Did you find out?" His hand grasped her shoulder. We pulled until she nestled in the crook of his arm.

"Yes. It was difficult, believe me. I thought about you all week. Every man I saw at work or on the street made me think of you."

"Then why didn't you call me? I couldn't get in touch with you. I don't even know your last name."

"Just for the record, my name is Samantha Arwood. Hearing from you only would have made the temptation that much more acute, so I'm glad you couldn't reach me."

"You like what we did together, didn't you?"

"That's what I'm trying to tell you. I liked it too much. I've never known a man like you. You're the only one I've ever met who can keep up with me."

"You've said that before."

Brooks smiled and touched the top button of her shirt. "Do you want me to try it again? Maybe it will be different this time."

She nodded.

———

They did try again, but the outcome was no different. The mattress in the bedroom served as a battleground. He made love to her until both were exhausted and drenched with sweat. After each session, when he had thought he had given her all that she could possibly want, she suddenly would recover and continue her demands. Now Samantha moved her head and kissed him on the chest, her tongue sliding out in a wet little point, moving teasingly between his nipples.

"I love your body," she said softly, caressing his shoulder and chest.

"I love yours, too," he replied and moved his hand across her smooth back.

She asked, "What are you doing tomorrow?"

"Why not stay?"

"I don't think I should. My mom doesn't like for me to stay out overnight."

"Couldn't you say you were at a girlfriend's?"

"I don't lie to her. If I told her anything, I would tell her I was staying with you, and take the consequences."

"Samantha, where do you live?"

"On the other side of town. We have an apartment there."

"Who's we? Mother, father, sisters, brothers?"

"No. Just my mom and me. I'm an only child and my parents are divorced. They have been for almost fifteen years." She kissed his chest again, this time her tongue working on the skin. She asked, "Does it make me a tramp to say I love your body and want it?"

"Not if you mean it. The flesh is just as special as the mind and spirit. I think your body is wonderful, and I don't feel guilty about thinking so."

She frowned. "But you're a man. It's different for you. Women aren't supposed to admire men's bodies or to enjoy sex."

"Maybe that's what I like about you. You don't feel guilty about lovemaking."

Samantha stirred uneasily. "Don't be too sure," she said. "I have my moments. It isn't always like this." She sighed. "I suppose you must have had lots of women. There are always women ready to love a body like yours."

"You would be surprised. No girl has inspired me the way you have or has done the things you do."

"I couldn't act otherwise."

"Are you trying to say you love me?"

"I don't know. I guess I love you as much as I can love anybody, but…"

He broke in, "Then you're saying that you don't?"

She shook her head. "I'm only saying I'm not sure. Let me ask you the same question. Do you love me?"

Brooks could not honestly answer her. There was something there, no doubt about that. But he did not think of his feelings as love. He had to admit that he liked Samantha's company away from the bed as well as in it. Did that mean he was serious about her?

"Love is really important to you, isn't it?" he asked, instead of answering her question.

"On the contrary, it's not important at all."

"I don't understand."

"Brooks, haven't you guessed the truth by now? The situation should be pretty obvious."

He frowned. "I still don't understand. I just don't follow you."

"I don't need love. I need sex. Do all your women ask you for more and more and more the way I do? I doubt it."

Brooks continued to frown. The thought that Samantha was sexually disturbed had not occurred to him, although certainly all the symptoms had been there. "Being passionate," he said, "doesn't mean you're insatiable."

"It isn't just passion, Brooks. It's more than that. I have made love with men, and it's always the same. No matter how much I get, I want more…" Sitting up, she began to rub her upper arms as if she were cold, causing her firm breasts to sway gently. "There's a name for women like me, Brooks. And not a very nice one."

"Cut it out," he said, sitting up and putting his hand on her thigh. "You're not a nymphomaniac any more than I am a satyr. Women of that kind can't derive any pleasure from the act. You certainly do. A lot of pleasure."

"Then why does my need keep plaguing me?"

"I don't know, Samantha. I'm not a psychiatrist. You have a strong sexual drive, but it's not abnormal."

"How do you know? You just said you're not a psychiatrist."

"You've been satisfied by me. That's how I know. The fact that you have a sizable capacity for love doesn't make you an oddity."

"I wish I could believe you," Samantha said, looking intently into his eyes. "You don't know how I wish I could believe you."

"I'd like to help you, Samantha, if you'll let me."

"What can you do? Make love to me all day, every day."

"You wouldn't be able to take that any more than anyone else could. But I will make love to you as often as you want and for as long as you need me."

She laughed. "Until you grow tired of me or until I wear you out. You don't know what you're saying. How long do you think you could keep up with me?"

"Would you care to find out?"

"It almost sounds like you want me to move in with you. Is that what you're asking?"

"It might not be a bad idea, for a start. Would you be interested in that?"

Samantha rose from the bed in search of her tossed aside clothing. Brooks watched the play of muscles in her firm bottom, feeling no real desire yet hypnotized by the tantalizing curves of her body. She came back and sat beside him, one leg curled under her.

"I've never lived with anyone before," she said. "I doubt that my mom would approve."

"Are you worried about that aspect of it or is it the idea of losing your freedom that bothers you?"

"Freedom to look for other men?" she asked, arching her eyebrows.

"I don't think you'll need anybody else."

She laughed lightly and kissed him on the chest again. "Are you bragging or complaining?"

In a sense it was a kind of courtship but it was a strange one. Samantha did not move in with him, but usually she would go to his apartment straight from her job, and they would have dinner together. Sometimes he would make one of the few dishes he liked to prepare; other times she would cook, although she had professed not to know much about the culinary arts. Afterwards they would talk, make love, and talk some more. Their lovemaking continued to consist of violent, prolonged sessions during which she tried to reduce him to a state of utter exhaustion. But their other hours together gave both of them as much, if not more, satisfaction. She was keenly interested in his work and always read his day's efforts before she left to return to her own home. He found her to be exceptionally perceptive and talking with her was often a refreshing experience. There were certain points on which they could not agree, and they spent many hours arguing. But these disagreements occurred mainly in the area of aesthetics, and usually debate ended with Brooks' statement: *De gustibus non est disputandum.* There is no disputing about tastes.

Some evenings Samantha seemed restless and even their lovemaking could not calm her. At such times, she tended to be hypercritical and disdainful. On two occasions she had not shown up until after midnight. She had been a little high and had seemed to take delight in flaunting her nakedness in front of him. He had written off such antics as childish defiance and so he had not been annoyed or angered very much. Still, he could not help wondering if she had been with another man.

Samantha never spent the entire night with him. No matter what the hour—even if it were four or five in the morning—she always would return to her own home.

It was a novel experience for Brooks. Never had he been so deeply involved with a woman before. He had come to consider her far more than just somebody with whom he could satisfy his physical needs. He eagerly looked to her arrival each night and tried to think of pleasant treats and conceits with which to surprise her, although she usually was not impressed by frippery of any sort whether material or intellectual. But he recognized a change in her as their relationship continued. She seemed to laugh more and to modify her cynical attitude toward life. The less bitter she became, the more his regard for her grew. One morning, after an especially pleasing night with Samantha, he began to admit to himself that he was falling in love with her.

The idea of love brought up the question of marriage. At first he shied away from contemplating it. She had mentioned other men, and often he wondered just how promiscuous she had been. But since she had known him, she had not been playing around very much, that was certain. He had been more sexually active since meeting her than ever before in his life. He knew that excess was supposed to debilitate men. But so far he had not found this to be true. He began each day's work mentally alert and physically at peace. Each evening he looked forward eagerly to Samantha's return.

Yet the prospect of marriage filled him with doubt. Would he be able to meet her demands over a protracted length of time? And what would happen if he could not? Would she then seek out other men as she had before meeting him? That unpleasant thought was one that could not be shrugged off. On the other hand, he was not sure that sex was at the bottom of her insatiable hunger. If he could win her confidence and get her to talk about herself, her real self, maybe the mental release would mitigate her sex drive. The goal seemed eminently desirable, and the more he thought of it, the more he felt it imperative to probe her secret heart.

For three weeks their relationship continued along the same course—daily visits, daily lovemaking, taking meals together, conversing, spending an occasional evening out. Then, on Sunday, they decided to go on a picnic along the river. Samantha wanted to change into Levi's first, so Brooks drove her home from his apartment.

"My mom will probably be there, and you'll have a chance to meet her," Samantha said.

Brooks was pleased. Samantha had not talked much about her mother, and Brooks was curious.

Samantha's home was a four-room affair overflowing with exotic pieces of furniture. There were lacquered screens, simulated Japanese prints, manzanita branches, Oriental carpets. Everything was the antithesis of what Samantha herself would have chosen. He had learned by now that her taste, in spite of her sensual nature, ran more to the uncluttered lines of modern furniture and simple decor. The furnishings, Brooks concluded, were of her mother's choosing, not Samantha's.

Brooks was in the living room examining a small porcelain dish when Samantha returned with her mother. "Jessie, this is the man I was telling you about, Brooks Erickson," she said.

"Hello, Mrs. Arwood," said Brooks.

"So, you're the one who's been taking up all of Samantha's evenings." Mrs. Arwood smiled broadly, displaying even white teeth, but there was a lack of softness and warmth in her face. She was a tall woman, an inch or so taller than Samantha, with short hair bleached blonde. She was probably twice Samantha's age, but her face and neck were remarkably free from lines. The chief indication of age was the worn look of her hands. She kept them clasped in front of her as if trying to hide the veined back with her fingers.

Brooks felt an immediate dislike for her. Her look was almost one of challenge, and he could not fathom the reason. But he smiled and tried to keep the conversation light.

"You have a pretty daughter. Can you blame me for trying to monopolize her?"

"I wonder if it's just her looks that attract you," the older woman said, still smiling.

"Don't be witchy, Jessie," said Samantha easily.

"I merely meant that I hope he appreciates your intelligence also,"

Mrs. Arwood said. "Samantha has told me you're a writer. I'm sure you recognize brilliance when you encounter it."

"I do," Brooks said. "I'm aware that your daughter has an exceptionally good mind."

Mrs. Arwood's smile faded. "I prefer to think of Samantha as more than just my daughter," she said. Brooks thought her bantering tone of voice was a little forced. "We have too much in common to be limited to a mother and daughter relationship."

Brooks nodded, indicating that he accepted her judgment in the matter.

"I'll let you two entertain each other while I change," Samantha said. "I won't be long."

"Don't hurry," Mrs. Arwood said. "I'd like an opportunity to get better acquainted with Mr. Erickson."

Samantha cast him a cautioning glance, then left the room.

"Sit down, Mr. Erickson. Would you like something to drink? Port?"

"I'm not much of a wine drinker," Brooks said, seating himself among the pillows on the low divan.

"No, you don't look like the type. You seem more like a whiskey man. Most fellows would give anything to look like that."

"You mean masculine?"

"Yes. Men try to appear strong and rugged, although few of them are. They're full of weaknesses and soft spots."

"All of them?" Brooks asked.

"Such an overwhelming percentage of them that it's safe to say all."

"What do you expect from a man, Mrs. Arwood? Maybe you expect too much."

"I expect only that a man be able to perform a man's functions— provide for his family, keep them happy in whatever way they find happiness, dominate and control their lives to their benefit and his. In short, Mr. Erickson, to be the master and not the servant."

Brooks said, "Those are quite exacting requirements. Not everybody feels the need to be a master. However, I understand the European man more nearly approaches that standard than American men."

"I have not known any European men, but the American men I've come in contact with leave much to be desired. Women in this country are far superior to them." She looked at him appraisingly, he thought, probably to see whether he would take offense at her statement. It was obvious to Brooks that Samantha's mother included him in her condemnation of the American male. He searched for something to say that would set the record straight.

"Has it ever occurred to you," he began, "that all the great composers, writers, painters, sculptors, and scientists were men? There are just a few women who achieved greatness in the arts and sciences. And even the greatness of those don't compare with the really great men."

She laughed derisively. "The discussion was about men, Mr. Erickson. Not..." She flicked her wrist to indicate the dismissal of the subject... "Pansies."

"Are you suggesting that only an effeminate man can produce great works?"

"It's true, isn't it? Aren't the really talented people you mention gay?"

"Not to my knowledge. There seems to be an erroneous opinion floating around, started by the homosexuals themselves, I suspect, that only gay people appreciate the finer things of life. That's just bunk. In fact..."

Samantha broke in, "Hi, people. Am I missing something important? From the little I just heard of the conversation it sounded very serious. Anytime homosexuality is brought into a discussion, the subject is either handled intellectually or derogatorily. Knowing Brooks, my guess is that you're being intellectual."

"Your Mr. Erickson seems to have a rather exalted opinion of the male species," Mrs. Arwood said. "But then most men do."

"Jessie's been expounding on her favorite subject, I gather," Samantha said, and laughed. It was a dry and brittle laugh.

Brooks was glad of the interruption. The brief conversation had been just a little more than conversation. It had seemed more like a contest of wills, and he began to understand Samantha's attitude toward him a little better. He stood up and looked at Mrs. Arwood.

"It's always interesting meeting a woman with strong convictions," he said meaningfully. "Maybe we can continue our conversation one of these days."

Mrs. Arwood tried to appear amiable, but her attempt did not entirely highlight her antagonism. Her smile was a little grim. "I'm sure we shall. Have a nice time on your picnic but remember where you are."

The remark puzzled Brooks the rest of the afternoon. He did not feel, however, that he should ask Samantha to explain.

4

THE MORNING FOLLOWING THE PICNIC, Samantha woke slowly with a feeling of tenseness. She always hated Monday morning. It was the beginning of sameness for her, the repetition of the old fears, the torture of her desires. Monday meant another week of working in an office, using all of her strength to control her emotions, forcing herself to follow the discipline that she had set for herself.

She lay in bed for a moment with her eyes shut, dreading throwing back the sheet and making the effort to prepare for the day. She thought of the time she had spent with Brooks by the river. As always when she thought of him, she felt a mixture of anticipation and indecision. She had not known anybody quite like him. In a way he upset her, although she could not explain why. She enjoyed being with him, and she appreciated what he could do for her sexually, but still there was something about him that made her want to break up their romance. It was as if he were too much man for her, though she had left his apartment several times with a vague feeling of dissatisfaction.

At last, she kicked back the sheet and swung her legs over the side of the bed. She stretched her hands high overhead and arched her back, thrusting her breasts out against the gauzy material of her nightgown. She could feel her nipples rub lightly against the material, and the sensation made her acutely conscious of her body. She exhaled loudly and headed for the bathroom, pulling the nightgown over her head.

Twenty minutes later she was sitting at the kitchen table sipping a cup of coffee and staring out the window at the street. She could hear her mother moving about in the other room, readying herself for the day. Samantha swallowed her coffee quickly and hurried to the door, picking up her small purse from the coffee table as she breezed through the living room. She called a cheery goodbye to her mother and left without waiting for a reply. All the way downtown on the bus she stared through the window, trying to ignore the fact that it was Monday, pretending that it was Friday and that she would soon be free for another weekend with Brooks.

She had been working for a trade magazine for more than a year as a combination of secretary and all-around assistant to one of the editors. She liked her job. It was not as glamorous as working on a consumer magazine, but to her it was more exciting, at least, than working for an insurance broker or a sales manager. She helped with the details of production, the editorials, planning the layout, and gathering information for stories.

She rather liked Walter Karnac, the editor, and they had had a cocktail together after work from time to time. Occasionally they had worked overtime together to get the magazine to press in time, but she had routinely refused to become intimate or even very personal with him. She knew herself. If she allowed him intimacies, she was certain, for one thing, it would have meant a drop in her opinion of him, and eventually could only lead to loss of her job. But she had realized that he was acutely aware of her as a woman and probably would have made advances if given the least encouragement. So, Samantha had always maintained a rather distant attitude toward Walter, although she was friendly enough with others, male and female, in the office.

When she walked in this morning to face Cynthia at the switchboard, Samantha was greeted rather coolly. Cynthia, at forty-five, had been with the company for twenty-two years. Although a handsome enough woman, she was rather prissy and did not approve of Samantha's voluptuous beauty. Samantha had not gone out of her way to try to be liked by Cynthia or anyone else, operating more or less on the principle that being liked or not liked the way she was had to be much simpler than trying to act in such a way that others would like her. She had more male friends than female in the magazine, but that was to be expected. A considerable number of the men had at one time or another tried to cultivate her, with an eye toward seduction. Some of the other girls in the office pool considered Samantha a threat and treated her accordingly. But many were quite friendly and enjoyed the skill with which she handled ardent males.

Walter Karnac looked up from his computer as Samantha entered the office. He nodded pleasantly and returned to his task: writing the weekly editorial. Samantha knew he would not be interested in exchanging any pleasantries until it was finished to his satisfaction. She stashed her purse in the bottom drawer of her desk and walked to the lounge to see if anyone had made coffee.

Phil Wallace was there, drawing himself back up from the urn. He looked at her with his usual sheepish expression when she entered. He had been looking at her in that same way since the time he had invited her to dinner, after which she had let him take her to a motel out of the county. He had been unable to live up to his extravagant promises, and Samantha had laughed at him cruelly when he had begged off from any further participation. Phil handed her the cup of coffee he had drawn for himself. She thanked him and returned to her desk in Walter's office.

Later in the day she went to lunch with Kristi Pine, the circulation manager's secretary, and listened with some alarm to Kristi's account of her weekend escapades. She felt rather responsible for Kristi's sudden awakening to life and love.

When Kristi had first come to work for the magazine, she had been a shy girl fresh from a small community college. Samantha had elected to take her under her wing. She had invited Kristi to go with her to a raffish nightclub, neglected to mention that most of the clientele consisted of homosexuals of both sexes. Kristi had been shocked at first, then impressed by the ease with which Samantha mingled and by the aplomb with which she made a date with one of the marijuana smoking musicians. The experience apparently had shaken Kristi loose from her preconceived ideas about morality. A few weeks later in a moment of confidence, she had admitted to Samantha that she had let herself be seduced by a bartender. Now the girl was indulging in every kind of sexual adventure. Samantha gave her a short lecture on the dangers of promiscuity—who should know better—and the two girls returned to the office.

During the afternoon coffee break, Samantha again went to the lounge. While she was sitting at a table alone, Jack Gaunt came in. He was the advertising director and from time-to-time made suggestive remarks about her figure; he made a habit of hinting in a not-too-subtle manner that he would like to have a date with her, although he never came right out and asked her for one. Samantha had thus far fended him off, remembering the unhappy episode with Phil Wallace in her promise to herself to keep her involvement out of the office. But she felt a warmth spread through her as he sat down beside her.

"How are you holding up under our current heatwave?" he asked.

"The same as everyone else. I'm wilting."

"I've got a free night. How about having dinner with me? We can go out to the Stagecoach where it is air-conditioned."

Samantha felt her tension increase. The meal was where Phil had taken her before they had ended up at the motel. She wondered if he had passed along any information.

"I have a date," she said, although the blood in her veins had begun to race. This was the first time, she was thinking, that Jack had actually asked her out.

"Another boyfriend?" Jack said, smiling insinuatingly.

"No, the same one."

"He must be quite a guy to occupy all your time."

Now Samantha was sure Phil must have spoken to Jack. She said distantly, "Yes, he is, as you put it, quite a guy." She thought of Brooks' strong body pressing down on her, and she wondered if Jack's body was as strong or as heavy or as relentless. She could feel her nipples stiffening against her bra. Guiltily she tried to divert her thoughts.

Jack Gaunt then said, "You know that all you have to do is say the word and we'll make a night of it."

"You're bragging," Samantha said.

But as she walked from the room she was aware of a warmth in her arteries and the looseness in her loins. Her hands were shaking by the time she returned to her desk. She was glad Walter Karnac was not in the office.

Samantha knew the symptoms. She tried to think of Brooks and the fun they would have together that evening. With a feeling of desperation, she called his cell, but there was no answer. Suddenly stricken by panic, she wondered if something dreadful had happened to him. At last, she convinced herself that she was being unreasonable and stupid. She continued to try to reach him without success for the rest of the afternoon.

Just before quitting time, Jack Gaunt put his head in the door to ask if she had changed her mind. For a brief moment she felt like taking up his proposition and demeaning him the way she had Phil Wallace. But she resisted and dialed Brooks again, still getting no answer. She felt hysterical, actually was in tears as she ran for her car. It seemed to take forever to get to Brooks' apartment.

When there was no answer to her ring at his door, Samantha stared wildly. By this time her body felt as if it was on fire. She did not know which way to turn. Was it really possible that he had suffered some accident? Was he trying to avoid her, get rid of her? Oh, where was he? She needed him. She needed a man. Now!

Samantha fought for control of herself. Fleeing downstairs, she pointed her car toward her own apartment, thankful that her mother was working late that night. There would be no necessity for talking or explaining her upset. She flung off her clothes and stood under the icy shower, hoping to cool off her heated flesh. Then she thought of calling Aaron for information about Brooks. Padding naked through the apartment after leaving the bath, she dialed Aaron's number. No answer.

Naked and angry, Samantha charged into her room and threw herself across the bed, silently cursing herself for not having accepted Jack Gaunt's invitation. She stroked her hands down her still feverish body. She dug her nails into her own flesh, hoping that the pain would drive everything else from her mind. But it did not. Her thoughts raced. Mental images formed, exciting her still more, lashing her. Finally, she lost all control of her emotions and began to scream curses and pound her pillow.

Her mother came home an hour or two later. Samantha said that she had already eaten, so there was no need to fuss.

Then Samantha took three sleeping pills and retired for the night.

Brooks' absence was the cause of their first violent quarrel. The next day, while he was sitting at the kitchen table eating a sandwich, the doorbell rang. Samantha came storming in after the lock clipped open.

"Where were you yesterday?" she asked through clenched teeth. "I tried to call you all day."

Brooks was more than a little surprised. "I went over to see Aaron," he said defensively.

"I called Aaron and he didn't answer," she said, still angry.

"I went over there from about noon until three. Then we went out for a drink. Why were you trying to reach me?"

"You're lying. Aaron works during the day."

"He didn't work yesterday. He played hooky. I repeat, why were you trying to reach me?"

"I needed you. I needed you terribly and you weren't around. Why weren't you?"

"You were working. What can I do for you in the afternoon?" Brooks asked, annoyed at her unreasonableness.

"You weren't home when I came by here after work."

"I know I wasn't. I…"

"Where were you? Out with another woman?"

"No, I wasn't out with another woman. We met an old friend in the bar, and we got to talking. I forgot the time."

"Then why didn't you call me when you got home?"

"I tried, but your mother told me you had gone to sleep. I wanted you to meet us at the bar."

"You're lying to me. You went out and met another girl and spent the night with her."

"Samantha, be sensible. Does it mean I'm cheating on you when you call me and I'm not home?"

"Yes. I know you. I know your capacities."

"Samantha, stop it. I can't hang around the house all the time just on the chance you might call me. What was so all-fired important about reaching me anyway?"

"I needed a man. And I depend on you to be my man. Why weren't you here?"

Brooks understood. He put his arm around her shoulder and tried to pull her to him, but she shrugged him away.

"No. You can't get around me that way. I went through hell last night. Not just because I wanted to make love. I was afraid something might have happened to you. I'd die without you... Oh, Brooks, darling." She began to cry.

He drew her to the couch and let her cry for a while, finally lifting her upright and handing her a tissue.

"What are you doing here this time of day?" he asked.

"I'm on my lunch hour," she sniffled.

"What I told you was the truth, Samantha. I was out with Aaron and a fellow named Rob Dickson. Rob gave me an idea that may mean a lot to us."

Samantha kissed him lightly. "Forgive me. I know I was being unreasonable. I just got panicky. I trust you. I really do."

After a few more kisses, Samantha returned to her office.

That night when she saw Brooks again the lovers' quarrel was forgotten, her passion was like the breath of a blast furnace. It left Brooks more than exhausted. It left him scorched.

5

TWO EVENINGS LATER, Samantha arrived at Brooks' apartment after work as usual and prepared a light meal. Later, when darkness had cooled the air a bit, they went into the bedroom and made love. Their passion spent, they lay nude and slightly apart trying to take advantage of the slight breeze coming in through the open window. Brooks put out his hand and touched hers as it lay on the oval of her stomach. He had been doing a lot of thinking lately. He was convinced that he knew the best course for both of them.

"Samantha," he said, turning on his side so that he could observe her facial expression, "I want you to marry me."

Her features tensed. "Marry?"

"That's what I said."

She stared at the ceiling. "That's sweet of you, Brooks." For a moment she hesitated; then she blurted, "As I told you, I love your body. But I've got to look at things realistically. How long can you last? Can your desire keep up with mine forever? I doubt it…"

"I think I'm capable of fulfilling your needs. I have proved it so far."

"Brooks, it's not that simple. I wish I could explain it, but I don't know quite how."

"Try."

"Well, take that quarrel we had the other night. I didn't tell you exactly what happened to make me so panic-stricken."

"What did happen?"

"A man invited me to have dinner with him. That's what happened."

"So why should that upset you?"

"To an ordinary woman such an invitation would be innocuous. But it triggered a sexual reaction in me. I knew he was interested in more than just having dinner. He wanted to make love to me and knowing that did something to me physically. I felt as if an aphrodisiac had been injected into my blood. I was afraid I would yield to him, but I wanted to be faithful to you. So, I called you. I needed relief, Brooks. When you weren't around to give it to me, it threw me into that panic." She laughed bitterly. "You just don't have any idea what a member of the opposite sex can do to me, Brooks. A man just has to look at me. I can recognize the expression in his eyes when he wants me. And the horrible part of it is, when I see the lust I want to give myself to him until he has had his fill of me, until he is screaming for mercy, in fact."

"I hope that wish hasn't come on you recently," Brooks said uneasily.

"It did the day I tried to call you. And other days—evoked by you—but so far you've always been around to take care of me when that feeling came over me. But will you always be there, Brooks?"

"I will be if you marry me."

"Oh, darling, can't you see? When you make love to me, it's not really you that's performing. It could be any man who happened to speak to me or look at me. Can you take that, Brooks?"

"I doubt it."

"Well, then?"

"Honey," he said earnestly, "I understand better than you think I do. You haven't talked much about yourself, as I've wanted you to, but you've told me before that you consider yourself a nymphomaniac victim."

"So?"

"So, I wouldn't have asked you to marry unless I thought I had a solution." He took her hand into his. "It was given to me by Rob Dickson, that guy Aaron and I were drinking with. Rob told us he was buying a lodge in the Coeur d'Alene area up north so that he could get away summers and escape the Boise heat, which seemed to be getting worse every year. Now, look, that put an idea into my head. I've been up there, and it's great. Once you're off the highway, civilization seems to be thousands of miles away."

"What good would that do us?"

"If what you say about yourself is true, then moving up there would get you away from temptation."

"We can't just run away and hide, Brooks."

"That's true. But it's not really running away. We can call it a change of scenery. It doesn't make any difference as far as I'm concerned. I can work any place and in a beautiful, restful area like that, I could probably accomplish more than I do here. It would be like living in Eden."

But there would be men around even there," Samantha insisted.

"I suppose so. It can't be like here, though. In a city as big as this you are confronted by countless men on the prowl. And you live with a mother who, I suspect, has much to do with your feelings."

"She has nothing to do with them," Samantha countered quickly. "It's just me. And I like the city life, Brooks. I wouldn't know how to act in the backwoods. I would long for the excitement, the nightclubs and the entertainers, the concerts—all the things the city has to offer."

"The woods can be thrilling, too," Brooks explained "There's a majesty about them, a magnificence that dwarfs the man-made wonders of the city. There's lots happening there, too. You just have to know how and where to look."

"I'm no naturalist," Samantha said.

"I guarantee you will be after you have been there for a while. You'll become so interested in the out-of-doors that you'll never want to return to civilization."

"I don't think it would work, Brooks. It sounds idyllic, but I'm not the right type for it."

After that, as the weeks went by, they would talk about marriage between bouts of lovemaking. The more she argued against it, the more convinced Brooks became that it was just the thing for them. He considered it the only salvation, since they had learned to be unable to do without each other, and he was convinced he could cure her of her sex mania. At last, she agreed to be his wife. They decided on a wedding date two weeks later to allow Samantha to give notice where she worked, and to give Brooks time to write for information about accommodations.

Brooks had never thought of himself as the marrying kind, but now that Samantha had accepted his proposal, he was tickled by the whole idea. He recognized that Samantha was disturbed—he refused to call her sick—but he rationalized that he could quiet her fears and divert her all-consuming sexual drive into sublimations that would yield peace of mind and tranquility.

A few days before the wedding date, Brooks received a visit from Samantha's mother. He had just finished writing a letter to his publisher when she arrived. He was quite surprised to see her, because he knew she worked at one of the department stores during the day. She stood in the doorway with a slight smile on her lips, her white-gloved hands clasped in front of her, her purse dangling from her arm.

"Good morning, Mr. Erickson," she said, her eyes flashing down over his bare chest to the worn Levi's that were his only article of clothing. "Could I talk to you for a moment?"

Brooks backed away from the door and allowed her to enter. "Nice to see you, Mrs. Arwood," he began. "I wasn't expecting guests, if you're wondering about the way I'm dressed."

"I don't believe I could be called a guest," she said, eyeing the room as she walked to the couch. "I understand I'm about to become your mother-in-law." She sat down on the couch.

Brooks sensed the hostility in the woman, which all the less inclined him to be friendly to her.

"I hope having me as your son-in-law won't be too much of a burden on you," he said, sitting down on a chair opposite her. His remark was speculative, designed to test opinions he had formed about Samantha's mother after his brief encounter with her.

"In what way? Financially?" she asked.

"I think we both understand in what way," Brooks said, taking another shot in the dark. "What am I going to be called? Your brother? Just as you try to pass off Samantha as your sister?"

Mrs. Arwood's eyes became hard. "Whatever are you talking about? Are you trying to say that I deny Samantha is my daughter?"

"Probably only to certain people—those unsure of your age."

Mrs. Arwood drew back her head as if she had been struck, and Brooks realized that he had hit closer to home than he had expected. But he also realized that he was being unnecessarily hostile. After all, he did not know the reason for her visit. Maybe she had come on a courtesy call, in a spirit of politeness, he thought, and suddenly felt contrite.

"I'm sorry," he said. "That was entirely uncalled for."

Mrs. Arwood opened her mouth as if to reply angrily, then clamped it shut and waited a moment before replying. "Apology accepted," she said. "I was hoping we could be on good terms, since we're going to be associating with each other."

"I hope we can be on good terms, but I doubt we will be associating very much. Samantha and I are moving north right after the wedding."

A frown creased Mrs. Arwood's face. "Whatever for?"

"I think a change of scene will do Samantha good. She's never known anything except city life. She'll gain by going back to nature."

"How primitive. But she never told me anything about this. When did you decide?"

"About the same time, we decided to get married. It wasn't easy, but I finally convinced her to give it a try."

Mrs. Arwood continued to frown. "You're making a great mistake. I hope you realize that."

"In what way?"

"Samantha is no country bumpkin. Only the city can satisfy her yearning for excitement."

"People can be excited by rural things."

"But Samantha needs contact with people. She'll be stultified by isolation, believe me."

"I think you're wrong about your daughter, Mrs. Arwood. I believe the city has been a little too much for her. You've raised her in one, that's true, but you haven't taught her how to cope with it."

"Are you telling me that I haven't done a good job of bringing up Samantha?"

I'm not in a position to say. The only thing I know is that Samantha is a sensitive person and that there's much in this life that disturbs her."

"You can't hide such a spirited girl In the backwoods. She's a rebel, Mr. Erickson."

"If she's a rebel, she must be rebelling against something. So far I haven't been able to determine what it is."

"The inadequacies of men. That's what she is revolting against," Mrs. Arwood said firmly.

"Are you the one who taught her men are weak?"

"I taught Samantha only what I know to be true." She leaned back on the couch now that she was on familiar ground. She crossed her legs carefully, as of calling attention to them, and Brooks had to admit they were attractive despite her age.

"I don't know you well enough to understand you," Brooks said, looking at the smoothness of her skin clearly smeared with cocoa butter. "Why are you so bitter toward men? I think you've done Samantha great harm by putting ideas into her head."

"All parents try to pass on their hard-won lessons and beliefs," Mrs. Arwood said, observing the direction of his gaze and smiling. "I will admit that you negate practically everything I've tried to teach her."

"How so?"

"I can't imagine what she sees in you. Do you have some hidden assets?" She looked at Brooks pointedly, a glint in her eye.

"Maybe Samantha didn't really want to believe what you told her about men, and I showed her what she wanted to believe."

"And just what was that? Something exciting? You must be quite a man."

Brooks shifted in his chair uneasily. "Exactly what are you after, Mrs. Arwood?"

She leaned forward, her arms crossed on her cross knees, her lips pouting provocatively. "You mean you'd be interested in finding out? I can be many things."

Brooks stared at her, reluctant to admit to himself what she might be suggesting. Her words had not really been committal, but there was a suggestiveness about them that gave him disturbing food for thought. He shook his head. "I wouldn't be interested, Mrs. Arwood," he said. "I think I already know too much about you."

"Stop calling me Mrs. Arwood. My name is Jessie. Since we're going to be related, the least we can do is get on a first-name basis." She rose and took a few steps toward him then changed direction and began to walk aimlessly around the room. Brooks had the impression that she was deliberately parading her charms. "You must be quite skilled at sex or Samantha wouldn't agree to marry you," she said, her back to him.

"I think there's more involved in our marriage than that," he said, becoming annoyed with her.

She turned to face him. "There's nothing more vital than sex," she said evenly. "You may fool yourself, but you don't fool me or Samantha. She knows it as well as I do."

"I wonder just how much you do know, Mrs. Arwood. You seem to be hung up on just one aspect of life."

"You put it bluntly," she said, standing before him. "But that's to be expected. Most men are animals. How much of an animal are you?"

Brooks rose to his feet. She was standing so close that his bare chest almost met her bosom. "That's something you'll never know," he said.

Mrs. Arwood put her palm on his chest and ran her hand in a short arc across his nipple. He backed away from her but she seized his arm.

"I believe you're afraid of me," she said, her expression challenging him.

"I'm trying to keep you from making a damn fool of yourself—and of me," Brooks said.

"Don't worry about that. I won't be the one who looks ridiculous," she said. "But I'm curious about what Samantha has found in you."

"Let's be frank, Mrs. Arwood. Are you trying to prove that you're still attractive enough to take a man away from your daughter?"

Mrs. Arwood pulled her hand from his arm and glared at him

malevolently. "You're being deliberately crude," she said. "I don't approve of this marriage at all."

"I didn't think you would. Are you afraid Samantha will find out that what you've been telling her about men is not true?"

"What have I been telling her about men?"

"I'm not sure. But I suspect that it has a lot to do with her problem."

"What problem?" Mrs. Arwood queried scornfully.

"Don't you know, Mrs. Arwood? You're her mother. Surely you must have suspected, with her out night after night, coming home late. What do you think she's been doing?"

"I'm sure I wouldn't know," Mrs. Arwood said haughtily.

Brooks laughed. "Yet you've referred several times to your daughter's vigorous interest in sex. You'll have to pardon me, Mrs. Arwood. I'm a working man even though my appearance would not seem to indicate it."

There was hatred in her look as she picked up her purse from the couch. "Samantha is being a complete fool. But she's old enough to know her own mind, so I won't prohibit this marriage. Take my word, though, she'll come back to me soon. Neither you nor any other man will ever be able to hold her. She knows men for what they are, and eventually she'll see through you and she'll come back to me. She needs me more than she does you. She can have her pick of men, but I'm the only person who really understands her."

Before Brooks could answer, Mrs. Arwood stormed from the apartment, slamming the door behind her. He stood looking after her for a moment, wondering how dangerous an enemy he had made by resisting her advances.

6

BROOKS AND SAMANTHA were married during the last week in July. They consummated their marriage that afternoon in his apartment. A couple of hours later they went to her home, where her mother, still wearing the dress she had worn to the wedding, stared balefully at them as they packed Samantha's belongings. She kept sipping Scotch all the time they were there, and from time-to-time mumbled that they would never make a go of their marriage. By the time they were ready to leave, her eyes had become watery and glazed, her mouth was twisted in the sneer.

"I hope you'll be happy," she said loudly.

"Mother, please," Samantha said patiently.

"I've told you to call me Jessie," Mrs. Arwood flared. "You've made your decision. Now get out of here."

It was the only disquieting note during that otherwise blissful day.

Brooks had heard from the Chamber of Commerce to which he had written that there were several lodges for rent and sale in the area. The chamber had referred him to Mr. Greenwood, a realtor in town. Brooks had thereupon written to the realtor, and the man had replied that he could recommend a sportsman's lodge for rent a mile or so outside village limits.

The day after the wedding Brooks and Samantha loaded whatever possessions they could into his car and made arrangements for their other belongings to be shipped by truck. The next day they left for Coeur d'Alene in Northern Idaho.

Samantha's traveling had been confined mainly to trains or planes going from one big city to another. The automobile ride entranced her. She drew childlike glee from her discovery of the prairies and the hilly farmland. But when they reached the timber districts of the north, she was awestruck. Brooks immediately noticed the change in her. Her pseudo sophistication and her cynicism seemed to drop away from her as if she was suddenly denuded of a previous experience. He was heartened by the way she reacted. He had had his doubts that she would really accept primitive isolation after a life spent in Boise, but her delight was so genuine that it gave him new confidence.

The village near where Brooks and Samantha planned to settle down lay fifteen miles off the main highway amid thick forest. It owed its original existence to a logging operation that had long since moved away. But the settlement had continued to prosper because of its advantageous location for vacationers. It became the fishing and hunting center of that part of the state.

The office of the realty company was little more than a clapboard shed. A middle-aged woman, dressed quite plainly, was typing from shorthand notes when Brooks and Samantha entered. She looked up and removed her glasses. Brooks introduced himself.

"Mr. Greenwood is out at the moment, but maybe I can help you. I'm Mrs. McCarthy. I've seen your email and Mr. Greenwood's reply."

"Then you know about the place he thought we would like."

"Yes," the woman said, rising and walking to the wall, on which was tacked a large, detailed map of the area. "It's a lodge, a handsome place just outside of town. It belongs to a Chicago man who used to come up here for the hunting, but he's been in Europe for some time. It has all the modern conveniences and I think you'll find it very comfortable." She pointed to a spot on the map. "Would you like to see it now?"

"Not right at this moment," Brooks said. "We just arrived. We want to find a place to spend the night and clean up a bit. Could you recommend a spot?"

"We have one hotel in town," Mrs. McCarthy said. "It's small and old-fashioned, but clean. Just walk down this block and turn left. Can't miss it."

"Thanks. We'll see you later."

The hotel was just as Mrs. McCarthy had described it, a small inn dating back to the Civil War. Samantha laughed when she sat down on the bed and heard it squeak.

"If we stay here very long," she said, "we're going to give the natives something to talk about besides deer."

Brooks sat down beside her. The bed squeaked again and this time Brooks joined in the laughter.

"I'll bet the drawers in the dresser stick, too," she said. "And that pier glass. I haven't seen one of those outside of a museum." She wrapped her arms around his shoulders, leaned back, and pulled him on top of her. "This village is out of this world. Living here will be like having a vacation in Fairyland." She smiled up at him, her eyes sparkling and merry.

"You're not sorry?" Brooks said, conscious of her body beneath his.

"Not now. I was worried, but I didn't know it was going to be like this. Oh, Brooks, I'm so glad you insisted I marry you. I'm so happy to be here. Did you ever see anything so beautiful as those woods? And that lake we passed—paradise!"

"I was sure if I could get you up here you'd feel like that. I hope you'll never be sorry." He buried his face in her hair and sought her ear with the tip of his tongue.

"Darling, darling." Her arms tight around his shoulders, and she arched your back, bringing her stomach up against his. "You know what I want you to do now? Consummate our marriage."

"I did. In Boise."

"That was Boise. Our marriage should be consummated here, too. After all, this is where we start our new life."

He grinned. "I'm convinced, baby."

As the late afternoon sun streamed through the open west windows and a fly buzzed about the room, Brooks removed Samantha's skirt, blouse, and ridiculously small bra and panties. Then he undressed himself and lay beside her on the bed. He kissed her thighs and stomach, working upward to her breasts.

Sliding her palms through his hair, curving her fingers behind his head to draw him closer, she let a moan escape her lips. Her arms tightened around him. He felt the heaven-granted spasm as she accepted him, enclosed him within her eager womanhood.

The completion of the union was quick and violent, building them with mighty force.

With her eyes closed and a thin patina of perspiration along her upper lip, Samantha smiled. "They must have heard us all over town," she said. "This bed is like a public address system."

Brooks grinned affectionately as he looked down at her sprawled body, so marvelously relaxed, so beautiful. She opened her eyes, sat up, wrapped her arms around his hips and pulled him to her.

"I love you," she said. She touched him and kissed him sweetly.

When they returned to the realty office, Mrs. McCarthy glanced at them and smiled. She drew a sweater about her shoulders, removed the key from her desk drawer and turned the sign on the front door to indicate that the office was closed. She followed Brooks and Samantha out to their car.

The lodge was attractive, all right, Brooks thought. Set back about a hundred yards from the road, it was surrounded by tall pine trees. The ground fell away sharply on one side, however, yielding a view to the west unbroken except for the tops of the pine and scattered cedars. Off in the distance they could see a river reflecting little glints of sunlight as it rushed over its bed of granite boulders.

The building had a wide fieldstone veranda bordered by a rustic wooden railing. Wide picture windows flanked the broad front door. The main room downstairs was immense, with a fireplace built into the north wall and a balcony on two sides reached by a stairway on the south wall. The furniture was rustic, inexpensive, but perfectly suited the decor. A small utilitarian kitchen and what seemed to be a serving pantry completed the downstairs. Three sunny bedrooms, facing the west, occupied the foreshortened second floor.

Brooks and Samantha both fell in love with the house the minute they saw it. The owner wanted to sell the property, but he was willing to rent it until someone came along who wanted to buy. Brooks immediately gave Mrs. McCarthy a check for the first month's rent.

The next day they moved in. After a trip to town for provisions, they went for a walk around the grounds surrounding the lodge. Encountering a fast-moving little stream about one hundred yards from the house, they followed it until they came to a jam of logs that stretched to the opposite bank. They walked out on the bridge-like formation and stood looking down into the clear water.

They could see the trout holding themselves steady in the current with little wavering of their fins. A dragonfly skimmed the surface of the water. A big fish shot upstream, his shadow a streak along the bottom. Then he broke through the surface, his mottled back and silver sides gleaming in the sunlight for a split second as he caught the dragonfly and splashed back into the stream.

After a while, Brooks and Samantha resumed their walk through the forest. The jack pines stood in clumps with sweet fern growing ankle-high among the islands of trees. The ground was soft and spongy: sandy soil and matting of pine needles. At one point they came over a slight rise and discovered another lodge. There was no one visible, but they saw a plume of smoke coming from the chimney. Not wanting to intrude, they backtracked and went downstream. They walked far past the limits of their own property, following the stream as it curved around the village. Suddenly they found themselves in a wide, swampy meadow bordered on the far side by more jack pines.

As they stood looking across the weeds and tall grasses, a voice yelled, "The road's back that way."

Startled, Brooks and Samantha turned. They saw a man holding a rifle in the crook of his arm. He was dressed in faded overalls, blue denim shirt and a sweat-stained felt hat. Jerking his chin over his shoulder, the man repeated, "That way."

"I know," Brooks said. "I'm Brooks Erickson, and this is my wife. We just moved into the lodge beyond the river."

The man grunted an acknowledgment and started to walk on.

"Are you having any luck?" Brooks motioned to the rifle.

"Luck? No, sir, I ain't having no luck at all. Haven't seen much to hunt," he said as he walked back into the woods.

The next few days were relaxing and wholly pleasant. Brooks found that he could write with greater ease in his new environment and the revision for his book progressed rapidly. Samantha had brought a sketch pad and charcoal pencils along with her, and while Brooks was working, she spent many hours trying to capture pictures of the landscape. The honeymooners also went on picnics, hikes, and at times they would wade in the swift stream. At night they would read, play cards, and listen to the playlists on their phones. Sometimes it was cool enough to use the big fireplace, and they would lie on the rug in front of the flickering flames and talk.

Mrs. McCarthy dropped by twice. The first time she came alone and chatted for half an hour or so about some of the local people. On her second visit she stayed only a few minutes, explaining that her son was waiting for her out in the car. Brooks immediately became worried when Mrs. McCarthy mentioned that the lad was twenty-five. He wanted no visitors who might capture Samantha's interest, not until he was certain that she was cured. When he escorted the woman to the door, Brooks caught a glimpse of the son, noting that he was good-looking in a sharp featured way.

One afternoon when Brooks' writing bogged down, he stopped work and hiked alone along the stream. As he approached the spot where the logs spanned the current, he saw a fisherman in waders standing in the water. Brooks watched as the man cast. The line, curving forward, dropping the bait into one of the deep channels near the weeds.

Brooks sat down on a fallen birch warm from the sun. The man whipped his rod for another cast, and this time there was a strike. The rod snapped to life and the man thumbed the reel to slow down the line as it pulled out in a rush. The line tightened dangerously when beyond the logs a huge trout jumped out of the water. The man lowered the tip of the rod to relieve the strain but the line suddenly went slack. He wound it back and then walked toward the bank, shaking his head.

He nodded without smiling when he saw Brooks seated on the birch log. He stepped out of the stream and opened his aluminum tackle box.

"A beauty," Brooks said. "Too bad he got away."

"He's a snob," He said with exasperation. "Most of the time he ignores my bait, but when he does take it, he always breaks my leader. He must have at least half a dozen of my hooks in him."

"What are you using for bait?"

"Grasshoppers. The old boy seems to have an affinity for them." He squatted down, opened a jar, took out a small brown grasshopper. "Are you the folks staying at the lodge?"

"Yes, we're renting it."

"I heard someone moved in. I'm poaching on your property. Hope you don't mind."

"Be my guest," Brooks said. "I'm not a fisherman, so you're not giving me any competition. My name is Brooks Erickson, by the way."

The man stepped forward, his hand outstretched. It was a small delicate hand. The man himself was small and frail looking, with a sallow complexion and dark eyes. He had a thick, untrimmed mustache.

"I'm Pierce Forrest," he said sitting down beside Brooks on the log. "I live in the house just over the knoll."

"Are you a permanent resident?"

"No. I have a practice in the city. But for health reasons, I spend a month or two here each summer."

"The practice? Are you a doctor?"

"Psychiatrist."

"That must be interesting."

"Interesting, yes. Rewarding, no - although it would be if my body were stronger. Then I could work full-time at it." There was a bitter tone in his voice, "but I'm getting personal, which is improper on such short acquaintance." The man stared past the younger man and pointed. "Is that your wife?"

Brooks looked down the stream and smiled. "Yes, she's probably come out to see what happened to me. I was only going to be gone a short while." He waved to her.

Samantha grinned as she approached the two men.

"Looks as if you found company," she said to Brooks.

"This is Dr. Pierce Forrest," he said. "My wife, Samantha."

"A lovely woman," the doctor commented. "I'm always envious of men with beautiful wives."

"Are you married, Dr. Forrest?" asked Samantha.

He smiled sardonically. "I'm afraid not. I can't afford it."

"I thought psychiatrists were all rich," Brooks joked.

"It's not the money I can't afford," he said. "It's the energy."

"I've never heard that excuse before," Samantha said. "What does energy have to do with it?"

As if she didn't know, thought Brooks, and waited for Forrest to reply.

"When you only have one lung," he said, "even a little exertion can leave you breathless."

"I'm sorry," Samantha said, her smile fading. "I don't follow you."

"That's understandable," the doctor replied dryly. "We've just met, and I haven't had time to acquaint you with my afflictions."

"Do you live near here?" Samantha asked, ill at ease because of his apparent sarcasm.

"Just over the hill. Anytime you have a nervous breakdown, give me a call. But please be sure it's genuine and not a mere tantrum."

"I don't have tantrums, and I think my nerves are in good condition," Samantha said.

Forrest looked at her sharply. "Are you sure? Just from my short observation, I would say you are a rather tense person, subject possibly to moods of depression."

"How can you reach those conclusions in such a brief time? Samantha asked.

"The nails on your right hand are considerably longer than those on your left. Do you bite the latter? And if I may be so bold, there is a slightly worn place on your sweater in the vicinity of your left breast."

Samantha's face suffused with color. She was aware of her habit of touching the tip of her breast with moments of stress when she was alone. She had noticed the loss of nap on at least three of her sweaters but she had not thought anybody else would notice.

"Do you always play detective with the people you meet?" she asked.

"A hobby of mine. Looking at your husband, I'd say he was a sedentary type, probably engaged in a solitary profession. He's an indoor man rather than an outdoor one. Yet he has considerable stamina, I would say."

Brooks laughed. "How did you arrive at all that?"

"You gave me the clues. Your complexion is too pale for you to have spent much time in the sun. Therefore, you couldn't be an outdoor type. When we shook hands I noticed that your grip was strong and that there were no calluses on your palms. And you seem to listen to what I said as if you were filing my words away for future reference. If I were to hazard a guess, I would say that you are a writer."

Brooks said, "Pretty slick, Doctor. Can you probe your patients' problems with such accuracy?"

"Most of my patients don't have troubles worth probing."

"You seem to be discontented," Brooks said. "Perhaps you should analyze yourself."

"I've already done that. It's one of the requirements of the job. And I have forced myself to recognize my limitations, especially my physical ones. If I seem at times to be a little bitter about life, you'll have to indulge me. In spite of my training, I'm not what you would call a well-adjusted person."

Brooks shrugged. "Why should you feel that you have to be as physically fortunate as other men? Haven't you heard it takes all kinds?"

"I realize it's a big world. But I resent being one of its weaker inhabitants. In this respect I am quite immature."

Brooks said, "You may not have the physical powers some other men have, but there is such a thing as mental strength. In that respect, I would bet you are superior to most of us."

Dr. Forrest gave him a try smile. "Don't be too sure about that, either."

A short time later the doctor went back to his fishing. Samantha and Brooks walked arm and arm toward their lodge.

"I don't think I like the doctor," Samantha confided as they strolled.

"Why not? He seems like a nice enough guy. Outspoken and bitter, maybe, but intelligent and friendly."

"I know. But I get the feeling that he can read my mind."

Brooks glanced at her. "Did you get the urge when you were with him?" he asked with concern.

"What urge?" She looked up at him innocently. "Oh, you mean… No. Dr. Forrest did not appeal to me that way. And I definitely don't like being analyzed without my permission."

Brooks accepted her reply without comment, but he could not help but wonder if she were telling him the whole truth.

7

BROOKS SECRETLY BEGAN to watch Samantha closely after her meeting with Forrest. He waited for the signs of discontent and restlessness, but on the surface at least she was her usual cheerful self. She spent hours walking and sketching in the woods. She cooked, cleaned, and frequently experimented with decorating the lodge. She seemed entirely content, quite free of the driving hunger that had plagued her in Boise. But her physical demands on him fluctuated widely. At times she was insatiable, as if bent on reducing him to emptiness; at other times her response was soft and trembling, as if she were giving her body rather than demanding his. This was a side of her that was new to him.

But for all her appearance of serenity, Samantha had begun to feel fears and doubts. She had told Brooks the truth when she had denied any desire for Forrest. What upset her was the fact that she was living where people were so few. If she should suddenly be overcome by her old sexual cravings and yield to some local man, everyone in town would probably know about it. She would not be able to hide in the anonymity of city multitudes and would bring shame to herself and to Brooks. The thought frightened her a little when she realized that just one moment of uncontrolled desire could ruin her. Sometimes, now, she felt antagonistic toward Brooks for getting her into such a difficult situation. Yet in her more charitable moments she felt deeply indebted to him for being concerned enough to risk his own happiness for her.

It was toward the latter part of the month that the lives of the newlyweds swiftly began to change. Brooks had said that he was going to drive to the city to see if he could find a book that had been mentioned in a review he had read. Samantha had declined the invitation to accompany him, saying that she planned to walk to town, do some shopping, and chat with Mrs. McCarthy.

After Brooks had left, Samantha hiked along the dusty road that led to the village shopping district. There she stopped at the old grocery store. She explored the merchandise for a considerable time, and by the time she was finished, she had purchased more than she could carry. The owner of the store offered to deliver the goods to the lodge. She agreed, telling him at what time she would be home.

Samantha continued to the real estate office, hoping to find Mrs. McCarthy available for a social call. She had nothing special in mind to talk about, but the woman was the most friendly person with whom Samantha had come in contact.

But Mrs. McCarthy was not there. As Samantha entered, a young man removed his feet from a desk and sat up straight. His sharp features were rather handsome, but a deep scar on his right cheek gave his face a sinister appearance. His pale blue eyes had a bold, calculating quality as he deliberately looked Samantha up and down.

"Is Mrs. McCarthy around?" Samantha asked, unnerved by his insulin stare. She already could feel the tension beginning to build up within herself.

The young man shook his head slowly. "She's out. I'm Gil McCarthy, her son," he said with a sly grin. "I'd be happy to help you."

"It's nothing important. I just dropped in to say hello." Samantha edged toward the door.

He rose from the chair and walked toward her. "You're Mrs. Erickson, aren't you?"

"That's right," she replied, hoping he would not come any closer.

"I saw you the day I took Mom out to the lodge. You kept looking at me through the window as my mother was walking to the car. Are you sure there isn't anything you want? I have a feeling I could help you out." He winked knowingly.

Samantha was incensed. The young man had lied about her showing any interest in him. However, his crude attempts at making a pick-up excited her. Suddenly the maddening need was racing through her body. She shook her head and backed toward the door.

"What's the matter, Mrs. Erickson? Afraid of me, or something?" He grinned crookedly at her. "I'm just trying to be nice."

"I think I'd better go," she said, reaching for the doorknob. "Tell your mother I was here."

"Yeah, I'll do that," he said. "But anytime you want special service, just call on Gil McCarthy."

Samantha turned and fled. All the way home she fought the torment. It was the first time since her marriage that the uncontrollable urge had come over her. The need seemed stronger than ever. She was trembling when she arrived at the lodge. She experienced the same feeling of desperation that overcomes an alcoholic when liquor runs out, only it was her husband, not whiskey, that Samantha needed.

But Brooks was away. He would not return until evening.

The last time she had that frantic hunger he had not been around either. She remembered the torture she had gone through on that occasion. He had married her to prevent a repetition of such suffering. Yet the first time the heat was on, he was not around—just as he had not been available then. Anger surged through her, but it could not blot out the other emotion. She began to pace through the house, cursing Brooks silently. Exactly when she needed him most, he was away, searching for some ridiculous book that caught his fancy.

She stopped beside his computer and looked at the pages of his manuscript. For a moment she had a childish urge to delete the whole file to punish him. It would serve him right if he had to rewrite the whole book. Just then though, she heard someone knock on the door. At first overjoyed, she thought her husband had returned early, but she realized quickly that if it were Brooks he would not have knocked. Then she thought it might be Gil McCarthy and she was terrified. Had he followed her home? She walked to the window and peered through the curtains.

She sighed as she saw a boy holding a box of groceries in his arms. His bicycle stood propped against a tree.

It was difficult for her to know which was the stronger emotion - relief that it was just the kid from the grocery store or anger that it was not her husband. Moving quickly, she threw open the door. The boy appeared startled by her violence.

"Hello, Mrs. Erickson. I've got your delivery," the boy said.

Samantha backed away from the door, frowning at him. He was not very old but he was tall for his age. He carried the heavy box of groceries with ease. His brown hair was sun-streaked and there was a row of freckles across the bridge of his nose. He seemed to be uncertain as he passed by her and looked about, as if wondering where he should go. Samantha pointed toward the kitchen and followed him as he made for it. He seemed to be mostly legs and a pair of shoulders, no hips, she noticed. Even while carrying the box, he demonstrated a kind of animal grace. An idea began to form in Samantha's fevered mind.

She stood behind the boy as he set the box on the cabinet. "What's your name?" she asked, feeling herself trembling.

"Ben," he said. "Ben Lowder."

"Where do you live, Ben?"

"Up on the hill."

"How old are you?"

"Eighteen. I'll be nineteen in another month."

Samantha walked to the refrigerator, keeping her eyes on the boy. "Would you like something cold to drink? You look warm."

"Yes, please. That would taste good after my ride." He fumbled for his pants pockets, not knowing what to do with his hands.

"Let me get you a Coke. It's a long way out here. Isn't it a little difficult riding a bike and carrying a box of groceries at the same time?"

"I got a basket rig. It isn't hard." As Samantha turned around with the open bottle, she saw his eyes rise quickly from her hips. She was wearing a pair of jean shorts and she knew that her hips and buttocks were clearly outlined.

She smiled slightly as she handed him the bottle. "Do you have a girlfriend, Ben?" She felt that if he looked closely, he could see her stomach trembling. Certainly, he could not miss her rapid breathing, her breasts heaving under the open throated white blouse.

Ben smiled self-consciously and shifted his feet as he accepted the bottle. "There aren't many girls my age around here. But I've got one who lives near the lake."

"Is she pretty?" She took him by the arm to lead him into the living room. "Let's sit down here where you can relax for a minute. Tell me about your girl."

Ben blushed. "She's really pretty." Samantha waited until he was on the couch, then took a position close to him, doubling her leg under her so that her knees touched his thigh.

"How often do you get to see her?"

"About once a week when I'm not working. But Mom says I'm not old enough to have a steady girlfriend."

"What do you think, Ben? Do you think you're too young?" She shifted her knee slightly until it pressed more firmly against his flesh.

But he seemed scared. He withdrew his legs slightly, "I don't know," he said. "If Mom says so, maybe I am."

Samantha patted his knee. "I don't believe you're too young at all," she said. "When you're not with your girl, what do you do?" She draped her arm on the back of the couch so that her hand hung a few scant inches from his shoulder. "Do you think about her? Do you think about other girls, too?"

He pulled hard from his bottle, not looking at her. "Sometimes," he said, embarrassed.

"In your thoughts, what do you do? Do you kiss them? Touch them?" She was becoming angry with him. He was a dolt. A stupid country lout who could not see a gift in front of his nose. She put her hand on his shoulder and closed her fingers so that her nails dug into his hard, sparse flesh.

Ben tensed under her grasp. He looked at her questioningly, his face becoming even more flushed.

"Are you afraid of me, Ben?" she asked, exasperated. She leaned toward him, parting her lips slightly.

But he drew back, his eyes transfixed by the approach of her throbbing red lips. He swallowed audibly. "I don't know, Mrs. Erickson. You're married!"

"What difference does that make?" Samantha said, angry at him for having reminded her of her status. She began to feel even more desperate because of his shy unresponsiveness. She put her hand on his leg and moved her face closer. Her lips touched his. Then he froze, holding his body stiff, his mouth flexed as she pushed the tip of her tongue against his compressed lips.

"Relax," she said, taking her mouth from his but not moving away from him. "I'm not going to hurt you. I'm going to show you what love is like." She kissed him again, moving her hand along his leg. She could feel him quivering but she was not sure whether it was caused by desire or fright.

"Haven't you ever kissed a girl?" she asked, taking his cold hand in hers. "Haven't you ever wanted to touch her here?" She placed his palm on the thrust of her breasts. For a moment Ben let his hand lie on her, too startled to move. Samantha pressed his fingers around one aching mound. All the pent-up fire in her seemed to flare and she pulled away from him. She yanked her sweater over her head, tossing it on the floor. She worked at the hooks of her bra, threw it off—shoved her naked breasts toward him.

"You know what these are for, don't you?" she demanded, rising to her knees beside him and thrusting her bosom into his face. "Haven't you ever wanted to play with them? Here?" she put a hand behind his head and pulled him forward until the throbbing, elongated nipple touched his lips. Ben tried to turn his face away, but Samantha clung to him, pressing into him until her flesh billowed against his mouth.

"Kiss it," Samantha said. "You must know how to kiss." She gasped as Ben's frightened lips closed on her flesh. Suddenly encouraged, she tore at his clothes.

When it seemed that she would black out from the torrent of passion that raged through her, Samantha pulled away from him and rapidly stripped the capris down over her hips, ripped off her panties. She flung herself at the boy, blind to his startled expression as he stared at her nude stomach and thighs. She worked frantically at his clothes until he was as bare as she. Gasping and moaning, then, she lay back, pulling him on top of her.

The boy was paralyzed with stupefaction. Despite his pounding desire, he could hardly move. Samantha cursed him but at the same time guided him. Even when her immediate goal was achieved, he did not seem to know what to do. She began to direct him with brutal, harsh words until he had to comply.

By then Samantha was divorced from herself, the person being gone and nothing remaining save the flame of her desire burning bright and hot. Gone was any consciousness of Brooks and her marriage. Gone were her fears of being exposed as a sex pot before the townspeople. Only her screaming need for fulfillment was important in that moment.

Suddenly she was aware of the boy's body going limp on hers. She bit her lips in despair, clung to him with her arms and legs, refusing to accept frustration. He struggled briefly, trying to pull himself away from her, but she would not release him. Her body continued to move in the invitation of its previous action until at last his own hips began to match the rhythm. A puppy dog cry escaped his lips as he buried his mouth in the curve of her throat and he completely gave himself to her demands.

When Samantha finally was through with him, she rolled away, her body slick with threads of sweat. For a moment she lay with her eyes closed as sanity returned. She opened them slowly and stared at the boy struggling to dress. His body looked small and pitifully thin, almost devoid of hair, browned by the sun except for the area of his flanks. The twisted expression on his face suggested that he was all but crying. He refused to meet her gaze.

The full realization of what she had done came to her. She sat up. The boy already was clothed and practically out of the house. She began to tremble with guilt and fear. What a terrible risk she had taken. Brooks might have come home early and caught her with the boy. That had not happened, fortunately. But if Ben decided to talk after his shock had worn off, she would become a marked woman. Certainly, word that she had betrayed him would reach her husband. On the other hand, she was already a marked woman. Gil McCarthy seemed to have sensed immediately what she was and this recognition has detonated her explosive lust.

After Ben had left, she turned on her side and buried her face in a cushion, wishing she were back in Boise where she could hide among the others in the growing city. Here she was exposed, vulnerable. Full of guilt, disturbed and by no means satisfied, she stood up, put on her clothes and began to pace the floor to quiet the trembling of her nerves. She poured a shot of whisky from a bottle in the kitchen cabinet and gulped it neat. She followed the first drink with three or four more. The alcohol did not do much for her nerves, but it did take her to the edge of drunkenness. She threw herself on the couch and began to cry.

That was how her husband found her when he returned home late in the afternoon. She looked up at him as he walked in and he saw her tear-stained face. He dropped the package he was carrying and ran to her. "Samantha! Samantha, what's the matter?"

For nearly an hour, with husbandly patience, he tried to get her to talk. She would not. Finally, she threw herself in his arms, still sobbing and wailing. When she had calmed down, she begged him to make love to her.

He did. And when they were through, she lay as if in a catatonic state, stiff, face completely devoid of expression.

Brooks heated a can of soup and fed some of it to her. She came to life, then, at least enough to smile weakly at him and ask for a glass of water.

Brooks watched his wife closely through worried eyes. "Now tell me, honey. What's wrong?" He asked softly, noticing that her breathing had returned to normal and her body was no longer rigid.

She could not lie to him, she thought. She could not lie to Brooks. "It happened again today," she said.

He knew what she meant. Clenching his fists, he growled, "The urge?"

"Yes. Marrying you and moving up here have not changed a thing. I'm still that way, Brooks. You were wrong. You can't isolate me enough."

"I'm sure I'm right," he said firmly. "But it can take time to get over a serious sickness. You've got to give yourself time, that's all. I'll help you. Of course, I've got to know the facts. Give me the whole story, from the beginning. It wasn't Forrest, was it?"

"Oh, no." Samantha put her hand over her eyes as she would not have to look at him. She inhaled deeply, nervously puffed smoke from her nostrils. "I stopped in to see Mrs. McCarthy, but just her son was there and tried to flirt. However, that was enough to set me off."

"What did he say?"

"Nothing special. It wasn't his words. It was the sound of his voice and, mostly, the way he looked at me. Oh, I knew he wanted me, Brooks. I could tell how he lusted for me." She began to weep again.

"Samantha," he cried an alarm, "you didn't let him…"

"Oh, no, Brooks. But I was afraid I would. I…fired up like a furnace. It was awful. I ran away from him, came straight home, and you weren't here. I tell you darling, it was torture. It drove me out of my senses!"

She did not tell him the rest of it. Not telling him about the delivery boy was not lying, she assured herself. It was less shame that kept her lips closed than fear of hurting Brooks, but in any case she could not force herself to disclose the degrading episode.

Brooks was badly shaken. He stroked her shoulder in an effort to comfort her and tried to show confidence. Yet he was already falling apart. What should he do? How could he help this beautiful but tormented creature who was his wife?

Eventually she fell asleep on the couch. Brooks covered her with a sheet. He marveled at the peaceful expression on her face as she rested. For a while, anyway, Samantha would be untroubled. He sat down in front of one of the picture windows, stared at the river off in the distance. The water playfully reflected the orange rays of the setting sun.

When Samantha awoke, it was past midnight. She rose, saw her husband silhouetted in the moonlight. He had not moved from the chair.

8

THE NEXT DAY Brooks left the lodge after breakfast to visit Dr. Pierce Forrest.

As he followed the stream through the woods, Brooks had some second thoughts. Would it be doing the right thing to discuss his wife's condition with a psychiatrist? The night before it had seemed a good idea, but right now he felt that it would be betraying Samantha. He shrugged away that thought. Samantha needed help. He was not being too successful at providing that help. The logical thing was to turn to someone with professional skills.

The psychiatrist's bungalow had a veranda running along the rear. As Brooks topped a small knoll he found himself on Forrest's grounds and saw him in a yoga position. The man's hands were folded in his lap and he was staring intently at the floor a foot or so in front of him. He seemed to be in a trance, and it was not until Brooks actually stepped up on the veranda that the doctor became aware of his presence. He craned his neck.

"Oh, Erickson!" he said, a smile replacing the slight scowl that had possessed his face. He unfolded his legs and pushed himself to his feet. "I didn't hear you come up."

"You looked as if you were contemplating the universe," Brooks said.

The doctor laughed. "As a matter of fact, my mind was blank. I'm training myself not to think at all. It's a difficult trip. Have you ever tried it?"

"You mean something like thought-control?"

"No. I mean blanking out all thoughts. It's a form of concentration. A meditation. As a writer you should try it."

"There are any number of things I could do to train my mind, but I'm too busy writing," Brooks said.

Dr. Forrest moved toward the door. "Come on in. After a session like that, I always enjoy a drink. How about you?"

"It's very early for me, but I'll risk it," Brooks said.

The interior of the house differed from the layout of the lodge. The ceiling was low. The furniture was solid and traditional. The living room walls were covered with groaning bookshelves. More reading material lay on end tables and in magazine racks. As he walked in, one of the volumes caught Brooks' eye. He glanced questioningly after the doctor, who was disappearing into the kitchen. Brooks strode across the room and picked up the book. As he had suspected, it was his first novel, *The Vile Thief*. He wondered if Dr. Forrest had purchased it after learning that Brooks was a writer.

He was still holding the volume when the doctor returned with two highballs. He laughed when he saw what the younger man held in his hand.

"I'm afraid I have a confession to make," Forrest said. "The minute I heard your name I suspected you were responsible for the book. My deduction that you were an author was based more on that suspicion than anything else."

Brooks laughed, took his drink, and sat down on the low couch. "It's a new experience, finding one of my creations in the possession of a relative stranger," he said. "I've seen them in the homes of friends and acquaintances, but never in the hands of somebody I don't know. Dare I ask what you thought of it?"

Dr. Forrest sat down in an easy chair near the couch. He held his drink in both hands. "It struck me as a light, competent, entertaining book. Rather superficial but honest."

"You must have read the reviews," Brooks said with a laugh. "That's more or less how the critics appraised my work." He took a sip of the drink, and added, "However, pleasant as it is to discuss my work, there's something else on my mind. This isn't a social call."

The doctor cocked an eyebrow. "Are you here for my professional services?"

"Yes."

"I was afraid our acquaintanceship would come to something like this," Forrest said. He tipped up his glass and drained it.

"Oh?" Brooks was surprised. "You expected it? Why?"

"It's fashionable these days to consult a psychiatrist. Authors are no different from anyone else."

"I'm not the problem. My wife is."

Forrest snapped to attention. "Go on."

"It's a delicate subject. I don't really know how to get started."

"Would you hesitate to tell your family doctor that your wife's bowels don't move?"

"No. But..."

"Then why do you hesitate to tell a psychiatrist that she has a sexual difficulty?" Forrest went on relentlessly.

"How did you know?" Brooks exclaimed.

"Otherwise, it wouldn't be so hard for you to talk about it. All right, now. Speak freely. Tell me everything."

Rather reluctantly, Brooks listed Samantha's symptoms, gave a full report of her behavior, and confided his reasons for marrying her and bringing her to this remote area.

"And did you really think you would be helping her by isolating her from men?" Forrest asked, annoyance clouding his face. "The untrained person playing psychiatrist is as dangerous as a child playing with a blow torch."

"I was doing what I thought would help her," Brooks said.

"Illness is no respecter of good intentions. You've got to get at the root of the person's problem in order to bring out a cure."

"But what could be at the bottom of it?"

"I haven't the slightest idea. And I couldn't possibly find out without talking to her."

"What would you suggest?"

"If you are convinced that it is serious enough, by all means get her to psychiatric treatment."

"Would you take her as a patient?"

"I don't think so. My practice is in another part of the country. It may take months or even years to get to the core of your wife's problems."

"I would appreciate it if you would at least give it a try."

Dr. Forrest rose and stood in front of the couch. "Does Samantha know that you've come to me?" he asked.

"No, I wanted to talk to you first," Brooks admitted.

"What makes you think she will want my services? Disturbed people rarely wish professional help. That's part of their disturbance."

"I'll talk her into it if you think it's the thing to do."

Dr. Forrest hesitated. "It may be a waste of time. Usually, it takes a number of visits for a pattern to begin to take shape."

"Is that always so, Doctor?"

"Not always, but you can't expect quick results. I want that to be clear."

"I understand. But except in this one respect, Samantha is a perfectly normal woman: intelligent, charming, completely healthy."

"In how many parts of the body does a person have to exhibit malignant growths to convince you that he has cancer? Before I say yes or no, I'd like to have a talk with her."

"Why don't you have dinner with us tomorrow night? You'll be our first guest."

Dr. Forrest chuckled. "I hope I'll be a welcome one," he said.

Returning to the lodge, Brooks was still wondering whether Samantha would consider what he had done a betrayal of her trust. He had talked to the doctor in order to help her, but would she forgive him on that account? He feared that she would not.

Brooks' worries materialized. When he told Samantha that he had invited Doctor Forrest to dinner, she seemed pleased; when he went on to explain why the psychiatrist was coming, she became bitterly resentful.

"Do you think I'm crazy?" she said furiously.

"Of course not. But if Dr. Forrest can help you get rid of your compulsion, why not let him?"

"How much did you tell him?"

"Everything I know."

"So how do I entertain a man who knows my sins?"

"Samantha, he's a doctor. He's not going to be sitting in judgment of you. He merely wants to talk to you in order to decide whether he can help you or not."

"Decide how much money we're good for, you mean."

"Don't be silly. Personally, I think he wants to find out just how much you want to be helped."

"Sure. He gets his kicks from playing detective."

"Samantha, be reasonable. You have nothing to fear from Dr. Forrest."

"I wish you had said something to me before you went blabbing to him. Why don't you mind your own damn business?"

"Anything that concerns you is my business." He put his arms around her shoulders and tried to pull her to him, but she broke angrily from his embrace.

"What's wrong with you?" She asked. "If you're so worried about me, you wouldn't make me miserable by spilling my personal details to the first person you can. What sort of an act am I supposed to put on for him? Shall I pant in heat when he looks at me?"

"Why are you so reluctant to talk to him? What can you lose?"

"What can I gain? All he'll do is ask me questions about my sex life so he can get a vicarious thrill."

"That's ridiculous, Samantha, and you know it. Why do you object to assistance? You've admitted that you have a terrible problem."

"I resent the intrusion into my privacy. I hate the thought of lying on the couch and talking about myself. Especially to such a weakling."

"Samantha, you're being unintelligent, and that's not like you,"

Brooks said. "Physical strength has nothing to do with being a good psychiatrist."

"Do you want another man knowing all about me and how you make love to me? Are you looking forward to that?"

"I'm only trying to help, Samantha. I want your mind to be at rest when you look at a man. That's important to me."

"Why? Are you afraid I'll cheat on you when you're not around? Do you want to be sure I'm your special property?"

"That's enough," Brooks said, on the point of losing his temper. "Dr. Forrest is coming to dinner tomorrow night, and I would appreciate it if you'd cooperate with him."

She looked directly at him for a moment, then made up her mind.

"All right, Brooks. If it means so much to you." She turned, walked up the stairs, and fled to their bedroom.

That night they did not make love.

9

WHEN DR. FORREST arrived at the Erickson's lodge for dinner, Brooks was relieved to see that his wife's hostile attitude toward the psychiatrist was not in evidence. She behaved exactly as though the guest was a mutual friend instead of a doctor who would be examining her with a clinical eye. Brooks had been a little apprehensive about the doctor's attitude as well. The man's outspokenness had a tendency to act as a stiff arm against any real friendliness. If he chose to be blunt with Samantha that night, Brooks reasoned, she might very well refuse to have anything to do with him.

But Dr. Forrest surprised them both. He was quite affable, regaling them with interesting anecdotes about the practice of his profession. Samantha entered into the conversation freely and appeared quite poised and calm.

After they finished dessert and were sitting before the fireplace, Samantha brought up the reason for the visit.

"Well, what do you think, Doctor?" she said with a smile. "Am I crazy enough to be put away?"

"I dislike the use of the word 'crazy'" he said, frowning. "I prefer 'emotionally disturbed.'" Dr. Forrest grinned mischievously. "But to answer your question, Samantha, you are nowhere near sick enough that you should be institutionalized."

"Then there's not much to worry about, is there? If I'm not disturbed enough to be sent to a home, there's no point in wasting your time with me. Right? I don't know why Brooks got so shook up he had to run to you."

"People who are disturbed seldom see why others are concerned."

Her cheeks flushed. "You mean, because I don't agree with him, that proves I'm insane?"

"Who said anything about insanity?"

"But anything less is nothing to worry about. Isn't everybody disturbed to some degree?"

"That's beside the point. A disturbed person is not always the best one to judge whether he is sick enough to require treatment or not. An objective opinion is necessary."

"And are you impartial?" she snapped.

"That's what a psychiatrist is supposed to be. Even though we have had dinner together tonight, I don't believe we know each other well enough for me to be subjective about you."

"Do you have any real friends, Dr. Forrest?" Samantha asked.

The man's dark eyes regarded her steadily. "There are a few people close enough to be called friends."

"Male or female?"

Dr. Forrest did not waver. "Male," he said firmly.

"Then how do you presume to treat my ailment when you have no familiarity with women."

"That's uncalled for, Samantha," chided Brooks. "Dr. Forrest is professionally trained. His personal life has nothing to do with the case."

"My apologies, Doctor," Samantha said, bowing her head slightly. "You and my husband seem to have this worked out."

"Let me correct you, Mrs. Erickson. Your husband and I have not worked out anything. Accepting my help, if I'm prepared to give it, would have to be a voluntary thing on your part. Neither your husband nor I can force you—or wish to force you—to subject yourself to my treatment."

"I thought you said I didn't belong in an institution," Samantha said defiantly.

"I did. But that doesn't mean you don't need help. Your antagonism at the present time would indicate that maybe you do."

"Then you're with Brooks? You believe I should use your services?"

"Peace of mind is a wonderful thing, Mrs. Erickson. If you would like to find it, I will be glad to assist."

"You're so full of platitudes tonight, Dr. Forrest," she said. "You struck me as a man who would be more original in his choice of words."

"The ability to phrase uniquely is reserved for the talented few. I hope you will accept what I have said even though you may not like the way it was said."

"Well, I don't know, Dr. Forrest. The idea of becoming your patient was sprung on me so suddenly I haven't had time to think about it. It may take me two or three weeks to decide." She smiled brightly. "Would you gentlemen care for more coffee?"

Brooks looked at Dr. Forrest and shrugged. There was an inscrutable expression on the doctor's face.

It did not take two or three weeks for Samantha to reach a conclusion. She made up her mind a few days later, after a trip into town. She went mainly for exercise, but while she was there she stopped in at the general store to pick up the mail. Three or four idlers were sitting on the front steps when she arrived. They shifted slightly to allow her to pass. They did not say anything or do anything, except smile at her knowingly. Then she saw one of the men wink at the others. The meaning of the wink evaded her.

A letter from Brooks' publisher was in their box. She stuffed it into her purse and passed the group again, being careful this time to look at no one. She had reached the outskirts of the village when she heard footsteps behind her. Someone grabbed her arm. She turned quickly and stared into the smiling face of Gil McCarthy. For a moment she stood frozen, then tore her arm free.

"Keep your hands to yourself," she said fiercely, backing away from him.

"Remember me?" he asked, still grinning at her, but making no move to touch her again.

"What do you want?"

"Are you kidding?" The young man said. "Hell, I just wanted to get acquainted. We live in the same town and we ought to be neighborly."

"I don't know you, and I don't want to know you," Samantha said emphatically.

"Baby, I sure have a need to be friends with you." He took his first step toward her. "And guess what? You feel the same way."

"Why should I want to know a piece of filth like you?" she retorted.

"You wouldn't ask that if you would let yourself go with me. I've got your number, baby." He put his hands on his hips, spread his legs wide apart, and laughed into her face. "You're my kind of woman."

Samantha turned, began to run, then slowed to a fast walk. After a while she glanced behind her and saw that Gil was following her. She began to walk faster, taking a few running steps from time to time, but the man made no effort to catch up. He kept pace a few yards behind her.

When Samantha reached the lodge, she burst into the living room. Her face was chalky and her breathing labored. Her eyes were wide with fright. Brooks looked up, saw her condition, and stood up abruptly. In a couple of steps, he was beside her, his arm around her shoulders.

"Samantha, what's wrong? Don't you feel well?"

"Mrs. McCarthy's son followed me home…all the way from town."

"Followed you!" Brooks yelled. "What else did he do?"

"I don't know. Nothing, I guess. But…" Samantha ran a shaking hand through her hair. "He may still be out there. He came right up to the gate."

Brooks walked to a window and pulled aside the curtain. McCarthy was standing in the road, staring toward the house. Blind with rage, Brooks wheeled, ran for the front door.

"I'll see about him!"

"Brooks, wait. What are you going to do? Don't start any trouble. He didn't hurt me or anything."

"Don't worry. I'm just going to get one thing straightened out with him."

By the time Brooks reached the road, Gil McCarthy had turned and started to walk back toward the town. Brooks followed. After a few paces, McCarthy turned, eyed his pursuer, then halted.

As Brooks drew closer, Gil McCarthy spoke. "Hi, neighbor." He was considerably shorter than Brooks, and thin to the point of frailty. Yet Brooks got the impression of an inner strength that could be dangerous.

"My name is Erickson," said Brooks. "I live in the house back there."

"Yeah, I know. I'm Gil McCarthy."

"Why did you follow my wife home?"

McCarthy's small teeth flashed in the sunlight. "What makes you think I was doing anything like that?" he asked.

The man's brash self-confidence infuriated Brooks. "She said you were. That's good enough for me."

"I was just walking in the same direction she was. That doesn't mean I was following her."

"You frightened her. She came into the house practically hysterical."

"I can't help it if she's the anxious type."

"You may try to shrug it off, but we both know the truth. You keep away from my wife. Understand?"

McCarthy's eyes became dark slits. "You listen to me," he said. "This is a public road. I have as much right to walk along it as she does. As long as I don't touch her or harass her, there's nothing you or anybody else can do to stop me."

Brooks knew that McCarthy was right. Momentarily he wondered if Samantha had exaggerated the situation, then he remembered the way this character had been standing in the road staring at the house. "I'm warning you, McCarthy. We don't want any trouble with you."

"I'm twenty-five and free to do whatever I want. I'll do what I please. But any trouble you have, mister, won't be from me alone. A lot of men are going to give you trouble. Once they get wind of your wife, that is. No matter how hard you try to play watchdog, they'll find a way to get at her, because in the end, she'll help them. I know exactly what she is."

Brooks felt ill. "What in the hell are you talking about?"

"Don't play dumb, Erickson. You know as well as I do what I mean.

And you're a fool for trying to keep a woman like that to yourself. No man can. Especially when she looks like your wife."

Brooks doubled his fists and moved toward the smirking McCarthy. "You dirty little…"

McCarthy quickly stepped backward and whipped out a knife from his pants pocket. He flicked it open. "Keep away from me." His eyes held the flat, deadly alertness of a man used to violence.

"All right, McCarthy," Brooks said. "You've got the knife. But let me tell you something. You bother my wife anymore and knife or not, I'll send you home to Mama in pieces. Do I make myself clear?"

"I see your lips moving, but I don't hear a thing."

Brooks turned on his heel and stalked back to the house. Although for a few seconds he half expected McCarthy to stick the knife in his back, nothing of that sort happened. He heard McCarthy chuckling but he did not look back. When he reached the walk leading to the house, though, he did glance around. McCarthy was gone.

Inside the house, Brooks found Samantha much relieved to see him. "What happened?" she asked. "Did you talk to him?"

Brooks nodded. "He denied following you, of course. He's a wise little punk, but I doubt if we'll have any more trouble with him." He decided not to tell her about the knife, or the things McCarthy had said about her. "How do you feel, Samantha? Did he affect you? I mean, are you excited?"

She looked at the floor, avoiding her husband's eyes. "Yes. I feel the same as last time. Oh, Brooks." She threw her arms around him and buried her face in his chest. "You don't know what it's like," she sobbed. "I haven't any control over it. I'm so… so damn disgusted with myself."

"Darling, that's why I talked to Dr. Forrest. You don't have to be tortured this way. Say you'll let the doctor help."

She shrieked frantically, "I don't care about anything right now except you and this feeling…" She tore at her clothes. "Brooks…please, darling…"

He sank with her onto the rug before the fireplace. He let her use him as she wished as she renewed her desperate attempt to rid herself of her compulsion.

Savagely, she demanded fulfillment. The wild match went on until her lust drained both herself and her husband.

The next day she agreed to see Dr. Forrest.

10

SAMANTHA DRESSED SLOWLY in preparation for her consultation. She dreaded the ordeal. She was still shaken by the meeting with Gil McCarthy and its aftermath, but not to the degree that she had been after the episode with Ben Lowder, the delivery boy. Although her debauchery always ended with her feeling deeply guilty, the affair with the boy had left her with more than guilt. She had gone into a depression deeper than she had experienced before. That condition of misery, indeed, had made her more vulnerable to the guilt and shame arising from the fact that such a horrible creature as McCarthy could trigger lust in her. So, she had consented to see Dr. Forrest. But the closer the time came to go to him, the more she regretted her decision. It seemed to Samantha that the promise had been wrung from her under duress, and she would be justified in not keeping her appointment.

Brooks watched Samantha as she fussed and puttered. "You better hurry," he said, realizing that she was stalling. "He'll be waiting for you."

"Oh, all right. I'm leaving right now."

"Want me to go with you?"

"I'd rather go alone, thanks."

Following the stream over the knoll, Samantha soon reached the doctor's bungalow. Fatalistically, she knocked at the door.

"Come in, Mrs. Erickson," he said, "I was beginning to think you had changed your mind."

"Almost, but not quite," she said, walking past him into the book-lined living room.

"It's a normal reaction. Won't you sit down?" He motioned toward the couch.

"I thought I was supposed to lie down."

"You don't have to. The idea is to get comfortable, that's all."

"The only thing that would make me comfortable would be to get out of here." She laughed nervously. "How do we get started?"

"It's quite simple. Just say what comes to your mind. This is a conversation that you are going to monopolize." His voice came from behind her and Samantha turned her head to look at him. He was standing a pace or two from the couch, staring down at her intently. "So that I won't distract you," he said, "I'm going to sit down here, behind you. I would prefer that you don't look at me when I ask a question."

"Why?" she said suspiciously. "Will you be doing something you don't want me to see?"

"I want to become a voice to you and nothing more."

"Okay, what do you want to know?"

"Anything you wish to tell me."

"How about starting with the details of that nasty childhood disease called bedwetting?"

"If it's important to you. However, as good a place as any to start is with your parents. Are they living?"

"I suppose so. Jessie is."

"Who's that?"

"My mother. She prefers that I call her Jessie."

"Why?"

"You'll have to get her on the couch to know the answer to that."

"Why don't you know about your father?"

"He deserted us when I was seven. We haven't heard from him or about him since my mother got a divorce."

"Do you remember anything about him?"

"Not much. Only that he never seemed to pay much attention to me. All I know about him, I learned from Jessie."

"What did she tell you?"

"Mainly that he was weak, that he didn't have the guts to assume his responsibilities."

"Is that why he deserted his family, do you think?"

"Probably. It seems like a pretty good explanation, doesn't it?"

The doctor said softly, "Tell me about your mother."

"She's quite young looking and attractive."

"Is that all?"

"Well, she's wild about exotic, romantic things. Ornate furniture, old pictures, rare materials, imported perfumes, incense, unusual lamps, and lighting. I don't particularly share her enthusiasm but they give her a lot of pleasure."

"Does she show any traits that strike you as masculine?"

"No. I don't think so."

"Then you would call her completely feminine?"

"Oh, yes. And so do her boyfriends, for a while at least."

"What do you mean?"

"They usually don't hang around very long."

"Have there been many of them?"

"There had to be. One man couldn't keep up with her for long. She may be feminine, but she is also very strong."

"In what way?"

"She winds men around her finger. She makes them do anything she wants. She is stronger than any of them."

"Did she ever consider marrying again?"

"No, never. Although there was one man, well, he lasted longer than the others. His name was Matt. A rather large kind man."

"What made you think your mother might marry him?"

"She talked about Matt more than she did the others. She seemed to have more respect for him. He had charm, good manners, and was a free spender. He was also very good in bed."

"How do you know that?"

"Jessie told me."

"Does she always discuss with you her relationships with suitors?"

"Don't get me wrong. We don't sit around and rehash gory details. When she does tell me anything, it is to prove her point."

"What point?"

"That men are weaker than women. And I believe her. We're supposed to be the inferior sex, but that's not true. Women are stronger than men in every way."

"Even physically?"

"Yes, definitely. Maybe not in weightlifting or things like that, but our physical endurance is greater than theirs. We have stronger wills, and we can withstand more pressure and pain before breaking down."

"Do you believe that it is necessary for the female to be stronger than the male?"

"Maybe it's not necessary, but it's a proven fact."

"Have you ever tried to compete with a man?"

She grinned. "Yes, and I've won almost every time."

"What form of competition?"

She laughed. "Sex rears its ugly head. I compete with men by going to bed with them. And from the first I saw that it was just as Jessie had said. They can't compete with us. We can outlast them all."

"Do you consider yourself stronger than your husband?"

Samantha hesitated. "I thought your interest was in my background."

"Your husband has become part of your background."

"We've known each other too short a time for him to have anything to do with why I'm here."

The doctor cleared his throat. "All right, Mrs. Erickson. I believe your difficulty is that you become highly aroused by the sight of men and have virtually uncontrollable desires to have intercourse with them."

Samantha gasped. Either Forrest was clairvoyant, or Brooks had told him even more than she had believed.

"Is that right?" snapped the doctor.

"Yes," she said meekly.

"How often do you get this compulsion?"

"It varies. Sometimes weeks go by without it. Other times it's two or three occasions a week."

"Do you always give in?"

Samantha nodded. "I simply can't do anything about it. When the urge comes over me, I lose the ability to judge or restrain myself."

"Have you ever noticed when the feeling occurs?"

"You mean what time of day?"

"No. Is it after a period of no sexual activity or when you're around a certain type of man or following a period of emotional disturbance?"

"I don't know. I never tried to pinpoint the circumstances. It just came over me, and I forgot everything else."

"Does it always occur when you first see or meet the man?"

"Sometimes. And yet there have been times when I knew the fellow for some time and then it happened. I can't explain why."

"Can you remember any of the men with enough clarity to describe them?"

Samantha thought for a moment. "Yes, I remember one. I saw him in the bar of a hotel in Boise. He was loud, boisterous, and laughed continuously; the type I detest ordinarily. But he attracted me - strongly and sexually. I tried to think of a way to meet him that wouldn't seem too obvious. I finally tipped over my drink and immediately he bought me another. After that it was easy. It took me less than an hour to get him out of there and into a hotel room."

"What was the result?"

"As it turned out, he was so inept that he was ridiculous. I had to laugh, which made him so angry that at one point he raised his hand to me."

"Can you remember any others?"

"There was a boy that I'd known for a couple of months. I met him through a group of friends who considered themselves Bohemians. They used to meet in somebody's pad, discuss religion, experimental art, listen to way out music and drink wine. This boy was a poet. He had no job. He was usually wearing dirty jeans and a sweatshirt. He had a scraggly beard and made no attempt to train it. One night he read some of his poetry. They were the most beautiful verses I had ever heard. His voice was soft and melodious, and the words just rolled from his lips. Before he was through, I could hardly control myself, I wanted him so badly.

We spent the night at his place, a grimy cubbyhole. I never saw him again."

"What happened in his room?"

"Do you want the juicy details or just a general description?"

"The description will suffice."

"He surprised me. He was gentle and quite controlled. Yet at the end he was no different from any other man."

"Did you have overpowering urges for your husband when you first met him?"

"Yes, but not immediately."

"Did you go to bed with him the night you met?"

"No."

"How do you account for that? If he produced the same feeling in you as these other men did, why didn't you make love?"

"I don't know. I can't explain it. I was strongly aroused sexually but when we got his apartment, I cooled off. That has never happened to me before. I went to the library the next day to see if they had any of his books. After I read one of them, I started to get the feeling again. I returned to his apartment. That time I didn't go home." She shifted her position on the couch.

The doctor asked, "Can you explain what your attitude toward your husband is now?"

She shrugged. "What would you expect it to be? We've only been married a month."

"How many times has this feeling come over you since you've known Brooks?"

"For men other than him, you mean? Twice while we've been married, and once just before."

"Did you go with the man who aroused you each time?"

"No," she said.

"Why did you hesitate?"

"I was trying to make a decision."

"About what?"

"How much to tell you."

"Describe the first time you had this feeling after you met your husband."

"I was at work. An executive asked me to have dinner with him. His suggested manner set me off. I refused because of Brooks. But I could hardly wait until I reached Brooks' apartment after work. When I got there, Brooks was out. That was a miserable night for me, I can tell you."

"Did you try to find another partner?"

"No. Strangely enough, I never thought of that. I thought only of being with Brooks."

"When was the second time?"

"When Gil McCarthy followed me home. Brooks was there, fortunately, and I directed toward him all the feelings this McCarthy person had aroused."

"Why should he create the need in you?"

"I don't know. He doesn't appeal to me. He's so mean and cocky. I'm actually afraid of him."

"And yet you felt attracted to him. Why were you afraid of him?"

"I don't know."

"Did he threaten you in any way?"

"Not exactly. But there seemed to be an implication in every word. I can't quite identify it."

"How about the third time?"

"What makes you think there was one?"

"You said you had this feeling three times since knowing your husband."

"I don't really remember a third time."

"What was so special about the third experience? Tell me."

Samantha stiffened on the couch and turned to face Dr. Forrest. He was sitting at a table by the window, his eyes fixed on her as if he were trying to mesmerize her. How could she bring herself to confess her seduction of the delivery boy? Forrest had no right to probe so deeply, to make her bring to light anything so personal and shameful.

"Why do you think there was anything special?" she said defiantly. Forrest rose abruptly. With his hands in the pockets of his sports jacket, he walked toward her. "I think that's enough for today. It's been quite a fruitful session."

"No. Answer my question," Samantha insisted. "What makes you think that third experience was special?"

"Your reluctance to talk about it. Maybe at another session you won't be so hesitant."

Samantha pushed herself to her feet and walked to the fireplace, passing within inches of him. "You think that it has something to do with Brooks, don't you?"

"I think nothing of the sort," Forrest said sternly. "I'm aware that you are reluctant to discuss your relationship with your husband. But I don't believe what happened on the occasion in question has anything to do with it. Let's wait until another time and you may feel free to unburden yourself." He rubbed his hand across his forehead. His eyelids drooped.

"Are you tired, Doctor?" taunted Samantha.

"I fatigue easily," he admitted. "Still, we have made progress today, and there's always tomorrow."

"What makes you so sure?" Samantha asked, putting her hands on her hips. "Are you positive I'll be around for another session?"

"Fairly positive." Dr. Forrest turned to face her. His lips were pulled tight under his mustache; his eyes were cold and direct. "I've been through this many times before. You are not unique, Mrs. Erickson. You belong to a category of humanity, just as the rest of us do."

Samantha's eyes widened. "That's the trouble with you headshrinkers. You have to categorize every patient. If you didn't you wouldn't know what to do with them. You have nice little pigeon holes created for you by Freud, Jung, Adler, and the others. If a person doesn't fit into any of them, you twist and distort until he does..."

The doctor shrugged. "Please, Mrs. Erickson. Today's session is over."

"Maybe for you, but not for me. So, you think I belong in one of your preconceived pigeonholes, do you?" Samantha paced the floor furiously. "All right. I'll tell you about the third time. It was special, you bet. And Brooks had nothing to do with it. He wasn't even there. He was in town looking for some stupid book. I desperately needed a man. My husband was not at hand so a teenage boy took his place. I had to teach the kid a lot, but he gave me what I wanted."

Dr. Forrest leaned against his desk, his hands still in his jacket pocket. "What's unique about that? Many women teach men to satisfy them."

"Not a man. A boy, I'm talking about," Samantha shouted, taking a step toward him, "not an adult who is supposed to have what it takes to satisfy a woman. A teenage boy. Don't you understand?"

"And did he give you what you wanted," Dr. Forrest said, without looking at her, "or did you take it? Was he just a convenient instrument, something for you to use?"

"He gave it to me," Samantha yelled, eyes blazing. "Which is more than you could do."

Now Dr. Forrest looked straight at her. "I'm no boy."

Samantha laughed. "Are you a man?" she challenged.

"Would you like a drink to relax you?" the doctor asked, pushing himself away from the desk.

"You think I'm lying, don't you? You think I'm saying all this to brag. Well, I'm not. It's true. Everything I've said is true." She grabbed hold of his sleeve and turned him to face her. "Do you believe me?"

The doctor pulled away from her. "Mrs. Erickson. I've said the session is over. I would be glad to give you a drink if you like, but I prefer not to talk about your problem anymore."

"Do you want to give me that drink to relax me or to get me drunk enough for you to seduce me?" she jeered.

"I'm sure if I wanted you sexually, I wouldn't have to get you drunk to have you," he said softly. He took her by the arm and turned her so that her back was to the couch. "Now, if you would like a drink, I will be glad to fix you one, otherwise I have to ask you to leave. I am fatigued."

Something in his expression stopped Samantha, and she sidled away from him. She put her hand to her chest, the tips of her fingers touching the worn spot on her sweater. The feverishness in his eyes did not abate and she felt suddenly uncomfortable with his hot stare boring into her. For a moment she thought taunting him with something obscene, but his look was so compelling that she said nothing.

"Good afternoon, Mrs. Erickson," he said firmly.

Samantha turned on her heel and headed for the door.

11

AFTER SAMANTHA HAD LEFT to see Dr. Forrest, Brooks continued to work for almost an hour. Then it occurred to him that there might be some mail in town. He donned his sunglasses and started walking down the road.

He never approached the general store that had the post office without smiling. In his reading he had encountered many descriptions of the village store, and this one was so typical that the similarity amused him. There was always a scattering of men sitting around on benches and on the steps. Most were smoking or drinking bottles of soda as they joked and made small talk. They were mainly the village loafers, who had no place else to go or anything else to do. This morning Gil McCarthy was one of those present.

He looked up as Brooks approached the general store, pausing with a bottle halfway to his mouth. His pale blue eyes were expressionless, without sign of recognition, but as Brooks drew abreast of him, he smiled.

"Good morning, Mr. Erickson," he said softly and quite politely.

Brooks was a little surprised. He wondered if McCarthy had undergone a change of heart. "How's it going, McCarthy?"

"Just fine," came the reply. "How's Mrs. Erickson? How come she isn't with you?" A small disdainful smile formed at the corner of McCarthy's thin lips.

Brooks realized his mistake. "She had other things to do," he snapped, starting to walk into the store. The other man stopped him by putting a hand on his arm.

"You didn't leave Mrs. Erickson way out there in the country by herself, did you?"

Brooks felt the eyes of the onlookers focus on him, and he glanced around uneasily. From the knowing expressions, he guessed that McCarthy had been talking about Samantha.

"Why?" He inquired, trying to keep his voice calm. "What business is it of yours?"

"None," McCarthy said with a mock look of surprise and hurt. "I was just asking to be polite." He turned to the other men and winked. "You gents will have to excuse me. There's something I've got to tend to."

He went down the steps and started walking up the road in the direction of the lodge. Brooks watched him for a moment and suddenly was filled with anger. He knew Samantha was not at the lodge, but McCarthy's implication was clear. Jumping from the porch, Brooks ran after McCarthy. He grabbed McCarthy by the arm and spun him around.

"Where the hell are you going?"

"That's no concern of yours, mister."

"Listen to me, McCarthy. I'm only going to say this once. If you go within ten feet of my wife, I'll kill you."

"I've got news for you," McCarthy retorted. "You folks aren't the only ones who live out this road. It so happens I might be on my way to see somebody else. So, you have no cause to try and stop me, the way you're doing."

Brooks said nothing, knowing that what McCarthy had said was true.

"But I'll tell you something, Erickson," the other went on. "When I'm ready for that dish we both know about, I'll get her. You won't know a damn thing about it, at least not until afterward. So go ahead and watchdog her. I can be patient, because I know that sooner or later I'll have her."

"You're insane," Brooks said. "I don't get it. What's the point of all this?"

"You got something that doesn't belong to you, Erickson. That kind of woman belongs to every man, and you know it."

"You're actually a lunatic," Brooks gasped, as if struck by a revelation. "Do you happen to know Dr. Forrest?"

"Forrest? What's he got to do with it?"

"I think you should talk to him."

"You city slickers can't outsmart me." McCarthy laughed. "You know what I'm going to do? I'm going to prod you into attacking me in public. Right now, a woman in that house over there is watching us. Someone like that will make a good witness. When you hit me I'll have you thrown in jail. Then what will become of your wife without you around to keep the wolves away? All I have to do is put my arms around her, and she'll fall like a ripe plum…"

Brooks fought to control himself. He could see the woman McCarthy had mentioned; she was standing on our front porch, watching them.

"You are sick in the head, McCarthy."

McCarthy was not listening. "Hey, I've got an even better idea! When I make you fight me, I'll kill you. It will be self defense, in front of witnesses. While you're rotting away in your grave, your wife and I will have a ball."

Brooks knew that if he stood there another minute, looking at that smirking face, listening to those insane words, he would take McCarthy's neck in his hands and not stop squeezing until the bastard was dead. He turned abruptly and trudged back to the general store.

As Brooks approached the steps, the loafers eyed him speculatively but none spoke. Brooks picked up his mail from the post office box and headed for home.

McCarthy's threats stuck with Brooks. He had not considered the possibility that if something happened to him Samantha would be left alone in this remote spot and, ironically, dependent upon only herself for protection from herself. The idea plagued him for the rest of the day and a good part of the night.

He did not mention to Samantha his encounter with McCarthy. When she returned from her visit to Dr. Forrest, she seemed strangely subdued. Brooks wondered what had happened at the session. He was not sure whether her attitude was a sign of progress or not. He would have liked to question her but refrained from doing so; he did not want to risk upsetting her.

There was no lovemaking that night. Samantha fell asleep quickly. Brooks lay awake for hours thinking about McCarthy.

The following day, taking a break from his work, Brooks walked purposefully along the stream in the direction of Dr. Forrest's bungalow. Worry about Samantha had been making Brooks restless and irritable. He was resolved to visit the doctor and find out from him whether any progress had been made. But as he came to the log jam that bridged the stream, he saw Forrest standing thigh deep in the water, fishing.

As Brooks watched, the psychiatrist had a strike. The line went taut. The rod bowed in a severe arc.

Looping in the line with his left hand, Dr. Forrest held his rod high. He tried to lead the trout toward him, fighting the current and letting the spring of the rod absorb the struggle. He shifted the equipment to his left hand as he angled the trout closer to his booted legs. He dipped his net into the stream, bringing it up under the twisting, convulsing fish, then lifted it out of the water. The doctor unhooked his catch and slid it into his creel.

Brooks had watched with admiration the skill with which the doctor had worked the fish. Doctor Forrest waded toward shore and hung the creel on the protruding root of a fallen tree so that his catch would be deep in the water. He lifted his hand slightly in salutation when he saw Brooks and slowly waded toward him. When he reached shore, and sat down beside Brooks, the doctor was breathing heavily. Brooks could hear a slight rasp with each breath.

"Much luck?" Brooks asked.

"Yes, I caught three large ones. They're hungry this afternoon." Dr. Forrest unwrapped a chocolate bar and offered it to his companion. Brooks shook his head.

"Dr. Forrest, how did it go yesterday?"

"You mean the session with your wife? Pretty well, for a starter. One or two things of possible significance came out."

"Can you tell me what they were, or would that be a breach of professional ethics?"

"Nothing of a very startling nature. There's obviously a strong maternal influence. Only natural, since her mother was the only parent your wife really knew."

"I'm sour on her mother, Doctor. She's a completely superficial woman, and quite mixed-up."

"How well do you know the lady?" Dr. Forrest asked, munching on his chocolate.

"I've met her a few times. I thought she tried to put the make on me one afternoon before Samantha and I were married. I suppose I could have been mistaken."

"You were probably right. From what your wife said yesterday, I'd gather Samantha's mother uses sex as a weapon."

"It wouldn't surprise me. She has definite ideas about the superiority of women over men."

"Yes, and she's passed on those ideas to your wife. How would you characterize Samantha's attitude toward you?"

"We get along pretty well together and have quite a few things in common."

"No, I mean, how does she act? Does she praise your work or make snide remarks about it? Is she affectionate with you?"

"She seems to like my books. She isn't wholehearted in her praise but she backs up her adverse views with good arguments. I wouldn't say there was anything snide or malicious about her criticism."

"Does she love you?"

"I would say so. She's not overly demonstrative but she is tender at times."

"Do you ever get into any discussions about politics, religion, ethics, anything really broad like that?"

"Our conversations are more usually concerned with personal matters like my work, our plans, our ambitions. We don't always agree. Now that I think of it, we rarely agree."

"Does she ever concede that you're right on a controversial issue?"

"No," Brooks said slowly. "Not that I can recall offhand. Is that important?"

"It could be indicative of any number of things, perhaps antagonism or a basic immaturity. I can't tell at this stage. She was reluctant to discuss her attitude toward you yesterday and that is also indicative. Have you had any difficulty in keeping up with her sexually?"

"I have a pretty healthy libido of my own," Brooks said with a smile, fishing in his pocket for a cigarette.

"It stands to reason," Dr. Forrest commented. He wadded the chocolate wrapper in his hand and shoved it into a pocket. Squinting up at the sun through the jack pines, he asked, "Do you like fish? To eat, I mean?"

"Very partial to fresh ones."

"I have a couple more than I really need. Why don't you have them for dinner tonight?" He stepped into the water to lift the trout from the root. He laid the creel on the water's edge and took a narrow blade hunting knife from a scabbard on his belt. Reaching into the container, he brought out one of the trout. He grasped the fish in both hands until he could secure a hold on it near the tail, then whacked it against the trunk of the overturned tree. The fish quivered for a moment and went rigid. Dr. Forrest laid it on the log and broke the necks of the other two trout the same way. He had laid them side-by-side on the log.

The doctor then cleaned his catch expertly. "Good eating," he said, as he placed the trout beside Brooks on the log. "I must get back." He waved goodbye as he started to walk off.

Brooks watched him disappear into the woods, then looked down at the fish. They had begun to lose their color and their unlidded eyes were becoming smokey. He noticed that the evisceration had been done with the skill of a surgeon—competent, clean, efficient—and he recalled for the first time that as a psychiatrist, Dr. Forrest must have had medical training. As Brooks rose to return to his own house, he saw the doctor's knife still stuck in the tree trunk where he had put it when he washed the fish. Brooks pulled it free. He ran his thumb along the edge. It was as sharp as a scalpel. He looked toward the knoll behind which the doctor's house was hidden, hesitated, and turned toward the lodge. He would return the knife another time. He hooked his fingers into the slits under the fish's jaws. Holding the doctor's knife in one hand and the fish in the other, he walked home.

12

SAMANTHA TWICE POSTPONED her appointment with Dr. Forrest. Finally, she made up her mind that she would see the psychiatrist again, no matter what, because her husband considered it the thing to do. Brooks had gone to town after exacting a firm promise that this time she would keep her appointment. But Samantha resented his insistence.

Once alone, she examined her body in the bedroom mirror before she began to dress. Her reflection was charmingly altered as she squeezed into the tightest skirt she owned and pulled on a blouse with a daring plunge. Both garments were white. She wore no underclothing.

She checked her image in the mirror and was pleased with what she saw. The skirt hugged her hips so tightly that every curve of her body was startlingly evident. Beneath the flimsy blouse could be seen the thrust of her nipples. She knew she was being vulgar; she was doing it for a purpose. If the good doctor was going to pump her about her sex life, she meant to give him something to think about while he was doing it.

She threw a cardigan sweater over her shoulders and started up the back way toward Dr. Forrest's house. She walked through the sweet fern and the jack pines. Her heartbeat accelerated when she was about midway between the houses and out of sight of both. For some reason she felt extremely excited, perhaps because of the way she was dressed. She pressed her lips as she started up the knoll that would bring her inside of the psychiatrist's bungalow. By the time she had reached the top, the palms of her hands were sweating, her loins felt loose, her breasts heavy and charged with heat.

When Dr. Forrest opened the door to her knock, he appeared more fatigued than she had ever seen him before. His eyes seemed more deeply set, and the lines running from his nose to the corners of his mustache were etched more sharply. He smiled slyly when he saw her and stepped back to allow her to enter.

"I've been working," he said, shutting the door behind her and walking to his desk. It was strewn with books and papers.

"Working?" Samantha scoffed. "I thought you spent all of your time fishing."

Dr. Forrest ignored the remark. "I've been preparing a case history that will be a classic. I expect to have it published."

"You mean you do something besides pry into people's sex lives?" She shrugged off her sweater and tossed it over the back of the couch. "Shall I sit or lie down this time?"

She turned so that he could see the deep cleavage between her magnificent breasts. His eyes glanced down at it, then moved to her hips. He motioned to the couch and took his place behind it. Samantha rested her weight on one foot so that a hip was outlined even more strongly.

"What part of my sex life would you like to hear about now?" she asked, smiling defiantly.

"Just say what comes to your mind."

Samantha put one knee on the couch and leaned toward the doctor, knowing very well that virtually the whole of her bosom would thus be rendered visible. "Tell me, doctor, what have you decided about me so far except that I've gone to bed with quite a few men?"

"It's a little too soon to be certain, but for one thing I'd say you have a definite hatred of men."

"Hatred?" she mocked. "That's priceless. I live to make love to men and you claim I hate them?"

"Are you sure it's making love? Were you loving those men, or were you just demanding them? To use making love as a euphemism for having intercourse is to grossly libel real love. In love there is a sharing. When just sex is involved, it can be and often is quite one-sided.”

“Then why did I marry Brooks?”

“I don't know. You tell me.”

“Because I love him. He's the strongest man I've ever met.”

“In what way? Sexually, mentally, physically?”

“In every way.”

“Then why did you force a delivery boy to make love to you?”

“I couldn't help myself. Brooks wasn't there when I needed him. I didn't want to cheat, but my husband let me down.”

“Did he let you down, or were you trying to hurt him in some way for not being available?”

“Isn't that the same thing?” Samantha said, annoyed by the doctor’s question.

“Not really. I suspect that you used the boy as a means of hurting your husband since you can't attack Brooks physically. He's a threat to the theory instilled in you by your mother, the thesis that women are stronger than men. You can't triumph over your husband any other way, so you tried to demean him by sleeping with another man.”

“That’s ridiculous,” Samantha flared. “I love my husband.”

“I wonder if you do, or if you are in awe of him and therefore a little frightened of him.”

“I'm not afraid of any man.”

“You told me that you were afraid of Gil McCarthy.”

“That's different. I'm frightened physically of him.”

“And yet he stimulates you sexually. Why don't you meet it head-on and reduce him as you've reduced the others?”

“Because I don't want to hurt Brooks. What kind of doctor are you to suggest that I commit adultery?”

“I'm not saying that you should. I'm merely asking why you don't.”

The nerve of this character, Samantha thought. He ought to be put in his place, but good. She straightened, thrusting out her breast. She brought her hand up to the clasp of her blouse and fingered it teasingly. “Does the idea of my committing adultery excite you, Doctor?”

She could not see his eyes, but when he did not answer immediately, she slipped the clasp open and stepped toward him. As if anticipating her intention, Dr. Forrest raised his hand and held it palm outward, obliging her to keep her distance.

"Excite me? Not in the least, Mrs. Erickson. Other men may find you sexually attractive, but I assure you that my interest is purely clinical."

"Don't you ever do any experimenting?"

"Never," he said, letting his hand drop to his lap warily so that he did not touch her. He leaned back in his chair.

"Are you afraid of me, Dr. Forrest?" Samantha said distinctly, moving closer. She felt her knees touch his leg.

The doctor cleared his throat. "It often happens that a person under analysis goes through a positive transference in which the doctor becomes a love object. I've been through many such situations. Yours is nothing new."

"That's what you think, Doctor. There's a lot about me that is different. Wouldn't you like to do personal research?" She pressed even closer, sliding her knees along his thighs.

Dr. Forrest tried to stand up but Samantha put her hand on his bony shoulder and pressed him back firmly. "Don't run away, Doctor. You maintain that people have to face things."

"Mrs. Erickson, sit down on the couch," Forrest said softly, straining against the pressure of her hand. "You don't know what you're doing."

"That's just your opinion."

She could see the doctor's face clearly now that she was next to him. His sunken eyes seemed to have lost their heat. His mouth was working nervously. A thin sheen of perspiration was on his forehead. She slid her hand under the material of his open-collared shirt; his flesh felt feverish and dry. She bent her head, then, and pressed her soft lips to his, feeling the coarse hair of his mustache. His teeth clenched against the intrusion of her tongue, so she drew his lips within her own. She loosened the top button of his shirt and sent her hand down across the chest. She could feel his breath against her cheek as his body heaved. She shifted her legs so that she stood astride of one of his legs. Her tight skirt was pulled up to her thighs. She kept working her pink tongue against his teeth and slowly his mouth opened to receive it.

Instantly she felt the glow of triumph and lowered her hips until she sat on his leg. The buttons of his shirt gave way before her experienced fingers and soon he was stripped to the waist. Still retaining the kiss, her tongue probing the inside of his mouth now, she continued to undress him.

All this while the doctor had been sitting impassively, allowing her to take the initiative. But when her hand explored his naked stomach, his body jerked. He closed his thin fingers on her breasts. He squeezed the tender mounds, causing her to cry out excitedly. Suddenly his arms tightened around her. With a strangled cry, he rolled with her to the floor.

Victory was in sight, and intently Samantha pursued it. She pulled off her blouse. The doctor tore at her skirt, fell on her, thrust her thighs apart with his knee. The man's contact with Samantha was brutal, unrelenting, But she experienced exaltation from the pain he inflicted. She drove herself up at him as he strived to beat her into submission.

He assailed her like a bull but at the finish he lost ground. He shuddered in a paroxysm that was like an epileptic seizure. Then he lay hopelessly still, his whole frail body trembling.

"Well?" She taunted. "That's all?"

He forced himself up from her and began to dress. She saw the crescent-shaped scar that began at his shoulder blade and disappeared beneath his armpit. Near it was another angry scar, a pale sunburst against the swarthiness of his skin. The effort of dressing seemed too much for him after the prior test of strength, and he collapsed to the couch, gasping, coughing.

"You seem out of breath," Samantha prodded sarcastically.

"I only have one lung."

Shocked, Samantha still stared at the telltale scars on his body. "Tubercular? Or, well, were you in an accident?"

"A bomb fragment found my chest cavity, back in the days when I was strong enough to do frontline surgery." He waited for his thudding heart to still, for his breath to return. "I thought I was still strong mentally, at least. But you, you've destroyed me."

"Aren't you being a little melodramatic, Doctor?"

"I've violated the ethics of my profession. I've betrayed my faith in myself, get out! Get out, damn you!"

Samantha rolled on her side, making no effort to get up. "Aren't we going to go on with the analysis?" she asked with elaborate innocence.

"I can't help you. Not now. You should be very happy about that."

"The great Dr. Forrest." She sat up and reached for her clothes. "The great doctor isn't quite so objective after all," she chuckled. "Oh, well, you did quite well considering your physical condition." She rose to her knees.

"You slut. You don't know what you've done to me."

"Yes, I do. I've just shown you that you're like all other men. Weak."

"You haven't shown me anything except your own sickness." He turned to face her, his thin chest heaving with his labored breathing. "You'll regret this, in time. Just as I do now."

She smiled broadly. "You shouldn't regret anything," she said. "A good loving is what a man needs. Will you agree now, Doctor, that I'm one of your more interesting patients?"

"One of my sticker ones, certainly."

"I wonder what I should tell my husband about our session today?" she teased. "Shall I say you're as vulnerable as any other man, that your professional training and your ethics and all that don't mean a thing?"

He turned away from her and walked across the room to a decanter of scotch on a table. He found a glass and poured himself a drink. "What you tried to prove today doesn't alter your case at all. You succeeded only in destroying my usefulness to you and perhaps my usefulness to anyone else. After what you made me do, how can I consider myself reliable as a practitioner? For that I damn you. If you believed in a god, I could curse you, but you believe in nothing except your own body."

"It's a beautiful, desirable body. No man can withstand it," she said arrogantly.

"You're right," he said, gulping down the scotch. "You can't stand it either. It will destroy you. Now get out of here. You've done enough damage for one day."

Samantha noticed then that there were tears in his deep-set eyes.

Suddenly sorry for him, she stood up and walked toward him, thrusting her naked breasts. "Don't feel bad. Despite your age and your wound, you performed as well as ninety-nine out of one hundred would."

He blinked back the tears. His eyes were filled with murderous hate as he gulped a second drink.

"And the other one percent, what about them?" he asked, sitting down at his cluttered desk beside the window.

"You would know about them," she replied, following him and resting one hip against the corner of the desk.

"I think I do. And I know your reaction to one of them."

"Who is that?"

"Your husband. You married him because you saw that it would take you a considerable time to dominate him, if you could dominate him at all. He's stronger than you are and therefore is a challenge."

"I married him because he can satisfy me," Samantha said angrily.

The doctor smiled. "You married him because you thought it would give you the time and opportunity to destroy him. That's the only reason. You don't love him. You're incapable of that emotion. Your body is a weapon that you use to degrade and therefore conquer, not inspire or uplift. You get your so-called uncontrollable urges when you meet a man with self-confidence, strength, one who might be your intellectual better or who might be an exception to your theory of female superiority. Your urge is to demean him, to destroy his self confidence in the only way you can—by outlasting him in a sexual marathon. How long will it take you to destroy Brooks? And how quickly will you leave him after that?"

"You're a liar. It's because he can match my strength, sexually and otherwise, that I love him and married him."

"Could be. You didn't give me time to find out. But it's far more likely," Forrest insisted bitterly, "that you latched onto him because you couldn't defeat him easily hoping to gain time to reduce him to nothing."

Samantha leaned across the desk, smiling into his face. "The way I did to you?"

Forrest's hand cut like a whip across her cheek. Stunned, she pressed the backs of her fingers to her face.

"I hope he is stronger than I, for your own good," the doctor said.

Samantha closed her fingers into a fist and pressed it to her mouth. "I love him. Nothing you can say will change that."

He closed his eyes. "Get out of here. Just get out of here."

Samantha turned from his desk. She pulled on her blouse and tucked it into her skirt. Then she threw a glance at Dr. Forrest.

A drink was trembling in his hand. His eyes were fixed on her. They were full of despair, failure, and horror.

The eyes completely unnerved Samantha. She backed toward the door and fled.

13

HURRYING through the jack pines and the sweet fern, Samantha soon was out of breath. She stopped in her flight and leaned against one of the trees. The day had suddenly become one of horror. Many times she deliberately set out to make a conquest of a man, but never had the result been quite like her experience with Dr. Forrest. She felt more like the vanquished than the victor. She pressed close to the tree trunk, the rough bark scratching her skin. She felt herself trembling fearfully inside and she wrapped her arms around the tree, trying to steady herself.

Not until the hand closed on her shoulder was she aware of another presence.

Frightened, she spun around to face the owner of the hand and looked into the smirking face of Gil McCarthy.

"Can't you find something better than a tree to rub against?"

"Get away from me," Samantha said.

"I'm not going to hurt you," he said, staring at the outline of her breasts under the blouse. "I want to make you happy."

"Go away. I'll scream if you don't go."

"Why fight it? I know all about you. That delivery kid told me."

Samantha choked.

"I can give you what you want," McCarthy said. "I've been waiting here in the woods for you."

"I won't have anything to do with you. You … you scum."

"And what are you?" He laughed and said dirtily. "We both know the answer to that, don't we? Well, I'm just the man for you, baby. Come here…"

He grabbed for Samantha, catching her by the wrist. She struggled but he managed to draw her toward him. Samantha could not move her eyes from his mouth as she strained to free herself. His lips, jerking and slobbering, approaching her face inexorably as he pulled her closer. When she felt his legs touch hers, she made one last effort to get away, swinging hard at him with her free hand. But he blocked the blow easily and yanked her to him, his mouth crushing down on hers. At the contact, she felt an overpowering rage, and at the same time an overwhelming desire not just to have sex with him but to conquer him.

In wild obedience to her emotions, she wrapped her hand around his neck, forced his mouth down even harder on hers, chewing at his lips in an effort to inflict pain. He released her wrist, savagely wrapped both arms around her so that his palms pressed her flanks. She sank her nails into the back of his neck.

"Ouch," he cried. "You bitch." He jerked away roughly, returned, threw his weight upon her, forcing her to the ground.

Samantha had the presence of mind enough to lift her skirt to her waist. She did not bother with her blouse, nor did he. He sent his hand along the smooth avenue of her thighs toward her belly. She felt his insistent fingers asserting themselves. She reached for him, tearing at his clothes. He was like every other man she had known, she told herself; she would soon put him in his place.

The union became a challenge for both of them. With fierce determination she clutched at him as he covered her. Her lovely hips crushed the sweet fern. She tore his shirt with her nails and beat on his back, determined to subdue him. McCarthy's answer was to stick his fingers deep into the soft flesh of those cushioned hips and match her drive for drive, his breath exploding in her ear. When his actions quickened, she felt the glow of victory. She redoubled her efforts and soon reduced Gil to lax immobility.

The moment he relaxed, she shoved him away and rose to her knees. She gazed down in triumph at McCarthy's panting figure. He no longer smirked. Rather, he had a look of satisfaction on his face. He rolled his side, propped his head on his hand.

"I wasn't wrong about you," he said, fumbling for a cigarette.

"Well, I wasn't wrong about you either, McCarthy," she said. "You're like all the others. You talk a good game."

"I took care of you, baby," he said, laughing softly.

Samantha jumped up and shook down her skirt. "You're good enough for whimpering little schoolgirls, maybe. You couldn't begin to satisfy a real woman."

"And that's what you consider yourself, I suppose. Baby, you're mighty pretty. But otherwise, you're like any other female, except that you like sex more. You can still yell uncle."

"Not by you," she glared at him.

"What makes you think you're so special?"

"I've met a lot of jerks like you. You promised a lot, but you didn't deliver."

He shoved out his arm and wrapped it around her knees, pulling her toward him. She stumbled but kept her feet. He sat up then and grasped the backs of her thighs, yanking her forward until she was standing astride his legs.

"Don't be so sure I won't deliver," he said, thrusting his face against the swelling of her thighs.

With a sharp pull he toppled her over so that her body lay partly on top of him and partly on the ground. Reversing their positions, he removed her blouse and lowered his mouth to her breasts. This time Samantha did not fight to get away. She set out with a vengeance to prove her superiority.

It was all over in a minute or two. When he rolled away from her, she turned on her hip and looked down into his face.

"What are you stopping for? Nobody said uncle yet."

He laughed between gasps. "You're great," he said. "Even better than I expected."

"You're all talk," she snapped contemptuously.

"Baby, you can say any damn thing you please. I got what I wanted. If you want to outlast me, you go right ahead. I'm getting my kicks...and you're not proving a damn thing."

Samantha released him abruptly and sat up. "You stupid little man," she said. "You can't satisfy a girl."

"You might be right." Gil laughed. "Especially your kind of girl. But I have a hell of a lot of fun trying."

Samantha jumped her feet and dressed. "Next time, don't try to do a real man's work."

She started walking away from him, down toward the stream, hearing his amused laugh following her. In spite of his derision, she felt vindicated, triumphant. She had not felt that way after her early episode with Dr. Forrest. She had known two men within the space of an hour and a half and she had subdued them both. One did not count for much since he had been a physical weakling, but the other had been a young man, a sexually strong man, and filled with confidence in his prowess. Reducing him to nothing had really proven her superiority over him.

She did not know what she was going to say to Brooks. The thought of facing him, knowing what had just happened to her, filled her with apprehension. It was the first time she had been unfaithful to him since seducing that boy, but there was a vital difference. With Ben she had not been able to control herself. With the doctor and McCarthy she had deliberately set out to be unfaithful. Of course, initially, McCarthy had forced her to submit; but after it had started, she had felt a compulsion to dominate him and had purposely egged him on. Dr. Forrest had been nothing. For all his big words and professional discipline, he had not been able to resist her when she had set out to prove to him that she was stronger than he. But she had more than humiliated him; she had really broken him up, destroyed him. What would Brooks say when he found out?

Her heart was beating rapidly by the time she breached the lodge. She paused inside of the doorway to catch her breath. Brooks was upstairs in one of the bedrooms, where he had set up his typewriter. Hearing her entrance, he rushed downstairs. He hoped Samantha would give him some indication of how the second session with a psychiatrist had gone.

Her appearance brought him to an abrupt halt.

"Hey! What happened to you?"

Samantha turned away from him, suddenly struck with the thought that her clothes were wrinkled and possibly grass-stained. She knew, too, that her hair must be unkempt. She glanced down at her blouse and saw that one of the buttonholes was torn. She covered the rip with her hand and crossed the room to the small kitchen. The liquor was kept there.

"I did some exploring in the woods. The brambles cut me up."

She poured herself a generous portion of whiskey and moved on to the window without looking at him.

"You look pretty sexy," he said jokingly, following her. "Do you have on a bra?"

"Of course not. You told me two or three times I'm a girl who doesn't need one," she said, still not looking at him.

"You must have given Dr. Forrest a real charge." He came up behind her, slipped his hands under her arms and cupped her breasts.

"Please, dear," she said, pulling away from him. "I don't feel in a sexy mood at all."

He frowned slightly, accepting the rebuff. "How was the head-shrinking today?"

"A drag. I don't think I'm up to any more of it. What a waste of time! He can't do anything for me."

Brooks' scowl deepened. "You haven't given it a fair chance, Samantha. You can't expect a change overnight."

"How long does it take to tell if someone is a phony?"

"You think Forrest is a phony? What the hell happened today?"

"Nothing happened. Nothing that's never happened before."

"Honey, you're acting very strange."

"If you don't mind, I'd like to take a bath, Brooks. I feel dirty."

Without waiting for him to answer, she climbed the stairs to the balcony, leaving him to look up at her as she crossed to their bedroom.

She kicked off her shoes and quickly peeled off the only two articles of clothing that she wore. She felt hopelessly, obscenely filthy, as if her body were covered with a layer of scales that represented all the sins she had accumulated.

She turned on the shower full force and tried to scrub herself clean.

14

THE FOLLOWING DAY, Brooks finished the revision. He packaged it and slipped it into an envelope and walked down to the village to get it mailed off. The writing had taken him longer than he had expected, but it had worked out pretty well. He was pleased with what he had done.

The store housing the post office was crowded with idlers, as usual, and among them was Gil McCarthy. He was talking to someone when Brooks entered but fell silent on seeing the writer. Brooks ignored him, making his way to the window to have the envelope weighed and stamped.

With that done, Brooks made for the door.

"What's your hurry, Mr. Erickson?" Gil McCarthy called. At the same time, he detached himself from his fellow loafers, taking a stand in front of Brooks.

The writer paused, then stepped around the smirking McCarthy without bothering to answer. McCarthy thereupon fell into step behind him and followed him out the door.

"How are things with your wife?" McCarthy asked loudly. There was a burst of laughter as the screen door slammed shut behind them.

Brooks turned furiously. "Look, punk. I don't want any trouble with you. Don't talk about my wife, and don't go near her."

"I don't think she wants me to stay away," Gil McCarthy said.

"You're getting close to having my fist jammed down your throat."

McCarthy laughed. "That's fine. Jam away. There are plenty of witnesses inside who will testify that you attacked me. That's all I need to jail you or maybe kill you."

Fighting down his seething fury, Brooks said, "Tell me something. What do you expect to gain? What is it you want from me?"

"Not a thing. I want it from your wife. She's the one who's got it to give."

"I've warned you to stay away from her. I'm not going to warn you again."

McCarthy chuckled. "Did you warn her to stay away from me? Where do you think she was yesterday afternoon?"

"I know where she was. She was visiting with Dr. Forrest." Brooks instantly regretted his words. He figured that McCarthy would immediately realize Samantha was getting psychiatric help.

To his surprise, McCarthy did not pursue that tack. Instead, he said, "Oh, she visited the doctor all right. But she didn't go straight home."

"I know that," Brooks said, remembering the exploration she had mentioned. "What's it to you? And where do you get your information? If you were following her again…" Brooks clenched his fists.

"Who was following her? I happened to meet her in the woods. After that, your wife and I had a very pleasant time together."

"What the hell would my wife be doing with a punk like you?"

"The same thing she would be doing with any other man."

"I don't believe you have the equipment."

"Ask your wife. She knows." McCarthy guffawed. And from the general store came the sound of more guffaws. The village loafers were having a ball.

Brooks blanked out for a moment. He did not disappear into the usual blackness of a faint. But he did drown in a sea of red, a turbulent and seething red.

Later he did not remember striking McCarthy. But he came to in time to see McCarthy stagger backward, tumble down the steps, crash to the paved walk.

Brooks took the steps in two leaps, lifted his hands in preparation for McCarthy's counterattack. But McCarthy did not get up. He had not moved since hitting the ground.

Brooks bent for a closer look. His tormentor lay face up, staring into the bright morning sky, blood leaking from the corner of his mouth.

The contingent of idlers rushed from the general store. One gaunt, blue-shirted man leaned over McCarthy and felt for a pulse.

"Somebody had better get a doctor," he yelled. "This boy is hurt real bad."

"He didn't have a chance," another muttered. "He got hit without warning. They were just talking when this man…"

"What's going on?" interrupted a second villager, who had rushed down the street and now it's pushing his way through the throng.

"This city feller hit Gil and looks like he hurt him pretty bad," the first man said.

The newcomer kneeled beside McCarthy and touched him. He listened at McCarthy's chest. After a moment he rose and stood looking down at the motionless figure. "He's more than hurt," he said. "Gil is dead."

Brooks' blood congealed. His mind whirled. In a fraction of a second, without even knowing it, he had taken a human life.

He stood paralyzed as the townspeople gathered around him in stunned silence.

"I guess maybe you better come along with me," the man who had announced McCarthy's death said. He was a gray-haired little man wearing a broad-brimmed hat and a week-old stubble of beard.

"Who are you?" Brooks asked, becoming frightened.

"I guess I'm the closest thing to the law in this neck of the woods," the man said. "The names Prolo, and I'm justice of the peace here."

"What do you mean to do?"

"I guess I'd better keep tabs on you until the sheriff arrives. I don't know whether this should be called murder or not, but Gil's dead. That's a fact."

The man's bony fingers closed on Brooks' arm. "Come across the street. We use Randy Bennett's store as a jail when we need one. It has a back room with a lock on it. I'm going to have to put you in there until the sheriff arrives."

Brooks compressed his lips. "Is there a lawyer in town?"

"There's Wiley. He covers most of the area around here. Can't say exactly how good a lawyer he is."

"Could you contact Wiley and ask him to come over to see me?"

"All right. I hope he's in town."

Randy Bennett's business, according to the sign over the door, was sporting goods. Primarily it was a bait and tackle shop. The interior of the small store was cluttered with showcases filled with artificial bait and tanks of minnows. A couple of racks help rods and tackle. The reels were on shelves. At the rear was a padlocked door leading to an even smaller room. The proprietor turned away from the front window of the shop as Prolo and Brooks entered. He looked suspiciously at Brooks.

"Morning, Randy," the justice of the peace said. "Guess we'll have to use the jail for a while."

"Was that Gil I saw him lying in the street?"

Prolo nodded. "He's dead."

"Dead?" The proprietor turns accusingly toward Brooks. "He do it?"

Prolo said, "Appears that way. How about opening up?"

Bennett walked to the rear of the shop, removed the padlock from the hasp, and pushed open the door.

"Please be sure to contact that lawyer," Brooks said on the threshold.

Prolo nodded. "I don't know whether he'll want to take your case though."

Brooks watched as the door was closed. He heard the padlock click into place. He rubbed his hand over his face.

Was he dreaming?

Surely he must be. All this could not be happening to him. He stared around the room, looked at the cot, the stool, the rusty little sink, the curtain behind which squatted an old-fashioned wooden toilet. A small, barred window high in the wall let in a glimmer of light. What the hell was he doing here, anyway?

The day had started like any other, and suddenly it had become a nightmare of unreality. That he had actually killed someone seemed utterly impossible. He had never been a violent man, subject to rages or outbursts of temper. But Gil McCarthy's taunting had been more than he could take. He had struck without thinking, without knowing, and now a man was dead. All because of Samantha, Samantha…

Brooks collapsed on the stool. Poor Samantha. He wondered what her reaction would be when she heard. It occurred to him then that he had asked for a lawyer but not for his wife. He felt guilty about it.

The minutes crawled. Brooks stood up, began to pace the floor.

He was still pacing an hour later when he heard the door being unlocked. A large and sullen man with a glowering expression walked in, leaned heavily on a cane, and dragged one of his legs. A cigarette dangled from the corner of his mouth. After he was in the room, he paused and stared at Brooks.

"I'm Wiley," he announced.

"Thank God," Brooks said, feeling a surge of hope.

The man nodded. "Jake Prolo said you wanted to see me."

"You know what's happened?"

The lawyer nodded.

"Can you help me? I mean I don't know what to do. I've never been in this kind of situation."

"Most people haven't. But I don't know whether I can help you or not. You're in more trouble than maybe you realize."

"I've killed a man. What could be worse than that?"

"You killed Gil McCarthy. That's worse."

"I don't follow you."

"Gil McCarthy happened to be a local boy, and his mother is well thought of in town. Besides, even though she works, her family has money. A lot of money. That means influence."

"Gil McCarthy was a punk. Maybe he didn't deserve to die, but he deserved a good beating."

"You're dealing with local people," Wiley said firmly. "The fact that you, an outsider, came in here and killed one of them is going to make things harder on you."

"But there was no premeditation in this," Brooks argued. "It was an accident really, not murder."

"Accident to you, maybe, but not to the folks around here."

"Will they try me?"

"You'll be tried somewhere in the county. They'll be on the jury. One of them will be the judge."

"What are you trying to tell me?"

"I'm saying that the best you can hope for is to get off with about five years for manslaughter. If it's considered second-degree murder, you'll get a much longer sentence."

"Are you serious?" Brooks exploded.

"Couldn't be more so."

"But I have a good defense. Now, listen, here's what happened…"

"Save it. We can go into that later if I'm your lawyer. I'm not sure that I want your case. Look, if you want me to retain someone else for you, I'll see what I can do."

"You mean get a lawyer from elsewhere? What good would that do? You said that people will resent me because I'm a stranger. Wouldn't they be even more difficult if an outsider defended me?"

"Probably. I'll leave that up to you." Wiley dropped his dead cigarette on the floor. "Just don't expect too much."

"But you do think my chances would be better if I retained you because you're a local man?"

"Frankly, yes. Thing is, as I said, I'm not sure I want to defend you."

Brooks snorted. "What kind of professional are you? I thought a lawyer is supposed to defend any person in trouble. Or do you interpret that to mean only those whose cases you think you can win?"

"You needn't get nasty," Wiley said calmly. "It would be my first murder case, but you get off easier with me than with anyone else. That I can guarantee. You wouldn't get off free, but you'd get a minimum sentence."

"Then will you defend me?"

"I don't know. But I'll stick by you through the preliminaries—the hearing and the indictment and all that."

"Thanks. That's something. Does my wife know what happened?"

"I have no idea. If you'd like, I'll go tell her."

"I wish you would. She's probably wondering where I am."

"I'll see what I can do about getting you out on bail, too. I understand they have already contacted the county sheriff."

"Bail? In a capital case?"

"A few states permit it, and this is one."

"How long will it take?"

"I don't know. Maybe tomorrow. I'll have to locate a bondsman."

"Fine. Meanwhile, please find my wife and get her in to see me."

"This is going to cost you," Wiley said.

"Of course," Brooks answered. "That's how lawyers make their money, isn't it? From the misfortune of others?"

Wiley's lips deepened at the corners, but he said nothing. His eyes on Brooks, he rapped sharply on the door with the head of his cane. The padlock rattled. The door opened and Wiley limped out.

Two hours later the door again was opened. Samantha burst into the room as if she were being shoved. She threw her arms around her husband and buried her head in his chest. Brooks was not sure how much of what McCarthy had said was true, but he knew his wife well enough to believe the worst. Nevertheless, he stroked her head tenderly, holding her to him. During this embrace, an enormous sadness possessed him. Flashing through his mind was a chalky face of Gil McCarthy lying on the ground, his sightless eyes directed towards the skies. It was Samantha, actually, who had put him in his grave - and had set Brooks up to pay the tragic price.

"Brooks, what happened?" she asked, her fingers clutching his shirt. "They haven't told me much. Is Gil McCarthy really dead?"

He nodded, wondering how he could explain that violence to her. In a moment of anger, he had violated his most cherished conviction, his belief in the sanctity of human life. Trying to play the role of Samantha's protector had led him to kill. What would become of her now? He moved his hand along her hips, cupping for a moment the fullness of her flesh. He held her close, feeling her breasts on his chest.

"Did you see McCarthy yesterday?" he asked.

"Yes, yes, I did"

"And did you get him to make love to you?"

"Brooks, no. It wasn't that way at all!" She hugged her husband fiercely. "He attacked me. He really did. When I was returning from Dr. Forrest, the rotten bastard ambushed me in the woods."

Brooks held her off at arm's length so that he could look into her face. "You didn't encourage him?"

"I swear I didn't. After he knocked me down, after he started to take me by force... Well, yes, then the feeling came over me. You know how I am. But he waylaid me, and grabbed me, and spilled me to the ground. Only then did I..."

"Never mind," Brooks said, and drew her close again.

Samantha lowered her head. "I know I should have let you know about it, but I was so ashamed. Did he...did he tell you? Brooks... Oh, is that why you killed him?"

"Not exactly," he said softly. He kissed her.

"I brought you to this. I did, didn't I?" Tears coursed down her cheeks. "Forgive me, Brooks. Darling, I love you. I love you."

"Sure," Brooks said.

He had taken pride, as a writer, in his understanding of human behavior, but clearly he could not understand his own. As he stood in that makeshift jail with his wife in his arms, he tried to evaluate his actions. Samantha's sex problem had seemed so simple, and he had been so confident that he could solve it. Had he been trying to play God? Remembering Forrest's comparisons of the lame man playing psychiatrist to a child with a blowtorch, Brooks cringed. He had been a fool to think that he could cure Samantha. For a brief moment he bitterly blamed her for the mess in which he now was involved. Yet he, not Samantha, had thrown the fatal punch.

"Samantha, darling," he whispered. "I'm not blaming you for anything, and I don't want you to blame yourself."

She lifted a cheerful face. "Will they let you off?"

"I doubt it."

"But a jury never convicts a man for killing someone who violated his wife..."

"This jury will," Brooks said. "They'll be on McCarthy's side."

"Brooks, no!"

Samantha crushed her fist to her mouth. She had brought herself and her husband to the edge of destruction. Yet all she could really think about was that at this moment she wanted him desperately.

Look at him, she thought. How calm and strong he is, amid all this trouble. Prison faces him, maybe worse, yet he's in full possession of himself. He isn't frantic or hysterical or anything. Oh, how I love him. How I want him. I wish you would throw me on the cot right now and take me…

For once in her life, Samantha fought down her boiling desires. Seething with inner fires, she kissed her husband and cooed to him affectionately, tried to comfort and encourage him.

When the padlock rattled, indicating that her time was up, Brooks had to admit to himself that he was devastated to see her go.

15

BROOKS WAS RELEASED on bail the second day. He was taken to the county seat and arraigned, then remanded to Justice of the Peace Prolo, who allowed him to go home. There was a definite coldness in Prolo's attitude as he assumed custody of Brooks, but the official stuck to the letter of the law.

Brooks had covered less than half the distance to the lodge when he saw the slender figure of Dr. Forrest approaching. He felt cheered at the sight of the man. Here was a friend. But then Brooks noticed something strange about the figure walking along the road. Dr. Forrest did not exactly stagger, but there was an infirmity in the walk that Brooks had not seen before. As they came abreast of each other, Brooks put out his hand and touched the other on the arm.

"Dr. Forrest, are you all right?"

The older man stared uncertainly into Brooks' face, apparently having some difficulty in focusing his eyes. "Oh, hello, Erickson. When did you get out of jail?"

"A few minutes ago. You know about the trouble I'm in?"

The doctor laughed foolishly. "Everybody knows. It's been coming through on the radio. What can I do for you? Need any therapy?"

For the first time Brooks realized that the psychiatrist was drunk. And from the looks of his disheveled clothes and unshaven face, Brooks guessed the doctor had been drinking steadily for several days.

"I have a feeling I should be helping you," Brooks replied.

The doctor cocked his head and stroked a finger along the shaggy line of his mustache. "You help me? That's a laugh. Well, if you mean it, go down to the village and get some more booze for me." He thrust his hand into his pocket. "Here, I'll give you the money."

"You know that isn't what I mean," Brooks said. He took Dr. Forrest's elbow. "Let me help you home."

The doctor jerked his arm free. "I can't go home. I'm out of booze." He seemed to suddenly remember something. "How is your dear wife?"

Brooks felt a surge of anxiety. "I don't know. I'm going home to see her now."

Dr. Forrest smiled. "Do that. Go home and make her happy before someone else does."

Brooks caught the implication. "You really are drunk," he said shortly.

"Now, how did you guess that? Oh, I forgot. You're an author and therefore a keen observer. You're right, I am drunk. And I've been drunk for days."

"What's eating you? What's driven you to it?"

"Ask your wife," Forrest said, turning away and starting to walk toward town.

Brooks grabbed him and stopped him. "What do you mean?"

"You fool," the doctor said. "You attempted to help your wife and made a mess of everything."

"At least I tried. That's more than anyone else did."

"You're so right," the doctor said bitterly. "You're the only one who was stupid enough to want to help her."

Brooks round. "Those are strange words coming from a psychiatrist."

"Don't call me that," Forrest roared. "The psychiatrist is strong and does not take advantage of other people's weaknesses."

"Have you hurt somebody, Dr. Forrest?"

The doctor shook his head. "I'm not like you, Erickson."

Brooks' face reddened. "I had no intention of killing Gil McCarthy, but he took Samantha sexually, then, flaunted the fact in my face."

The doctor shrugged. "Well, I haven't killed anyone. But your wife did. She killed me!"

"What are you trying to tell me?" Brooks shouted.

"For years I prided myself on my strength of will. I lacked a strong body but compensated for it by developing a strong mind or so I thought. But your wife destroyed everything. Do you understand?"

"No, I don't."

"Well, that's not unusual. It's customary for the husband to be the last to know," the doctor said, waving his slender hand in the air.

Brooks suddenly felt cold. Of course. He should have known.

"You slept with Samantha, is that it?"

Dr. Forrest began to laugh. "Of course, you fool. If I hadn't, do you think I'd be standing on a dirt road, drunk, talking to you this way?"

Brooks wanted to strike Forrest as he had struck young McCarthy, but he held onto himself with iron restraint. "Go on," he said. "Tell me the rest."

"What more is there to tell? Do you think the McCarthy boy was the only one to take advantage of your wife's condition? I made hay with her when she came to me for professional help. I violated the basic rule of my profession. I not only failed to help her, but I also harmed her. I said a while ago that I didn't hurt anybody, but that was a lie. I may have ruined Samantha completely." Dr. Forrest ran a hand through his unkempt hair. "And I let her destroy me, too. She pulled me down…" he turned defiant eyes on Brooks. "Do you understand me now? You brought her up here to protect her from herself, and in the short time she has been here, she has ruined my life, your life, and did she tell you about Ben Lowder? She used him, too. You should see him now. You killed Gil McCarthy because he was arrogant and full of pride. Well, are you going to kill Ben Lowder, too? He has become unbearable. Your wife has been the cause of one Gil McCarthy being removed from this world and another taking his place."

"Who is this Ben Lowder?"

"A delivery boy. She's been loved by at least three males in this vicinity: a seventeen-year-old boy, a physical weakling, and an obnoxious punk. That's your wife, Mr. Brooks Erickson. That's your Samantha." The doctor shook his arm free of Brooks' hand and stumbled on for the village.

Brooks watched him, trying in his horror to assimilate what had been said. It seemed impossible. The fact that Samantha had given herself to Gil McCarthy had caused him to commit a crime, and now he had learned of two others with whom she had been unfaithful. How many more were there? He turned toward the lodge and walked along the road, his thoughts spinning crazily. The girl was too sick. Too sick, he told himself. His poor wife was terribly sick.

Samantha met him at the door with a cry of pleased surprise. She threw her arms around his neck.

"Thank God, you're home," she said. "I need you so much."

Brooks drew her close, feeling hopeless and ineffectual. Everything he had set out to do had boomeranged completely. The girl he had wanted to help was beyond his help, beyond the help of anyone. What could be done for her? What would become of her?

"You feel so good," Samantha said. "You look so calm and strong. Make love to me. Help me forget the days we've been apart." She moved her hands down along his flanks and pressed against him.

Reluctantly Brooks let himself be pulled toward the stairs. But her need was so great that she could not make it to the bedroom. In the middle of the living room, with the hot, unfiltered sun streaming in on them from two sides, she fell to her knees and began to pull at her clothes.

"Help me," she said, turning stricken eyes up to him. "Help me."

Brooks dropped down beside her and put his arms around her waist. She was not satisfied with that. She twisted him until he lost his balance and toppled over backward. He clung to her, as she wanted him to, but with no feeling of wanting her. It was as if all sexual desire had died within him and he was left with only a profound pity. But he willed himself to meet her demand.

At long last she lay sprawled and exhausted, her eyes closed.

Wearily Brooks pushed himself to his feet and stood for a moment looking down at her, at the faint smile on her relaxed mouth.

"That was so good, Brooks," she said without opening her eyes. "What would I ever do without you?"

Yes, he thought. What would she do? While he was in prison, she would ruin lives right and left, that's what she would do.

Brooks moved away from her, going into the small kitchen and pouring himself a drink. He's sipped it neat, leaning against the small built-in cabinet. He noticed Dr. Forrest's knife lying on the cabinet top, where it had been placed after being retrieved from that tree. Idly Brooks picked it up and ran his thumb along the razor-keen edge. It was sharper than he had remembered, and there was a little flicker of pain as it sliced through the outer layer of skin on his thumb.

Samantha appeared in the doorway, smiling, looking charmingly disheveled. "Don't I get one?" she said, motioning at his drink.

Without answering, Brooks took down another glass, poured an ounce or two. Through the window above the sink, he could see the sun sparkling on the restless river. There was a call of a jay in the cedars outside, and a whisper of a breeze threaded the jack pines to come through the open window.

"Come here a minute," he said, still facing the window.

Samantha came up beside him and followed his line of vision. "What are you watching?"

"Just look out there," he said. He stood behind her for a moment, letting her search for what he wanted her to see.

The knife was very sharp and when it went in, it missed all the bones and penetrated deeply. Only a faint intake of breath marked the violence that took place inside her as the steel reached her heart. She arched her back stiffly, then began slowly to sag away from him. He caught her in his arms and gently eased her to the floor. Her eyes were closed, and her lips were slightly parted, but there was no movement to her breast. She looked more at peace than he had ever seen her.

He held her for a long moment, feeling the warm, sticky wetness flooding his hand on her back. Then he lowered her the rest of the way to the floor. He washed off his hand at the sink and left the lodge to report to Prolo.

THE END

ACKNOWLEDGMENTS

First, this book would not have been possible without my grandpa's capable knack for telling a good story. Growing up, I found out he was secretly publishing books under the name Max Collier. He passed away before I even knew he was a writer or had a chance to get the history and stories behind his alluring career. I decided to bring to life his original stories, previously published in the 60s and 70s under the veil of a brown paper bag in the convenience store.

A big thank you to my family who supported my decision to re-share these stories with you and continue to vote on their favorite cover choices.

A huge shout out to my editor Anna McHargue and Words With Sisters. Without them this project would not be nearly as fun and would definitely take twice as long.

Thank you to Fusion Creative Works for their skills to create fun and cohesive cover art designs.

As always, I'm so appreciative of Adriel for making sure this book was formatted correctly for you to have the best reading experience.

And to The Harmony Group for literally bringing harmony into my life so I could pursue my dream of being a published author.

ABOUT THE AUTHOR

W.B. Ford is an author living in Boise, Idaho who writes modern
retellings of books
published by Max Collier.
www.wbfordbooks.com

***

Interested in joining our Advanced Reader's Team? Apply today!

Sign up for my newsletter to be the first to know!

Last but not least, all reviews are greatly appreciated! Please share your
thoughts on this book (and all the rest) on your favorite reviewing
platform.

facebook.com/laurentylerauthor
instagram.com/blondierocket
goodreads.com/laurenctyler

ALSO BY W.B. FORD

Chloe

Leah

Eva

Samantha

Along Came Cathy

PUBLISHED AS LAUREN TYLER

Spark: a guide to kickstart or reignite your creativity

To Those Who Came Before

Maxton

Austen